if NOT me then WHO?

A romantic saga

ABHIPSHA PATTANAIK

BLOOMSBURY
NEW DELHI • LONDON • OXFORD • NEW YORK • SYDNEY

BLOOMSBURY INDIA
Bloomsbury Publishing India Pvt. Ltd
Second Floor, LSC Building No. 4, DDA Complex,
Pocket C – 6 & 7, Vasant Kunj,
New Delhi 110070

First published in India 2026

ISBN: 978-93-69520-26-8

2 4 6 8 10 9 7 5 3 1

Printed and bound in India by Gopsons Papers Pvt. Ltd., Noida

For every heart that has loved, broken,
and yet bravely hoped again.

4 January 2021

MADHAV

Hi, I'm Madhav, and this is a not-so-love but kind-of-love story of my best friend, Hriday. The guy who fell for the girl of his dreams, Arohi. Sounds simple? Yeah, it isn't. Life had its own spicy script ready for him. So buckle up, because this tale is full of love, heartbreak, jealousy, friendship, and a truckload of emotions.

"Maa, have you packed my tiffin? I'm running super late!" Hriday yelled, hopping on one foot as he tried to put on his sock and shout at the same time.

"When are you *not* late, beta?" his dad Raghuvir muttered from behind the newspaper.

"Here it is!" called his mom Maya, handing over the tiffin with one hand and holding back the bus driver's patience with the other. "Go fast! The driver has been honking like he's in a wedding procession!"

"What's for lunch, Maa? Aloo parathas, right?" Hriday grinned.

"It's dhokla today, beta. Now *go*, or else even the driver will eat your share."

"*Maa!* You always betray me at the last moment. I wanted aloo parathas! I'm not going today. I'm on a tiffin strike!" Hriday threw a dramatic tantrum.

"If you don't leave now, I'll eat your dhokla and still not feel guilty," Raghuvir warned, folding his paper.

"Fine, but for tomorrow, I want biryani!" Hriday pouted, giving his mom a cheeky wink.

"I beg you, Hriday, just go! The neighbours will call the police because of this honking!" Maya sighed.

Hriday finally sprinted out and climbed onto his school bus, which read "Shadley Public School, Rajouri Garden, West Delhi".

Now, every morning on that bus, Hriday had just *one* goal, spotting Arohi.

She was his "Yash Raj heroine", his mountain-dancing muse. In his head, he often danced with her in Switzerland, under snowfall, in slow motion. Yes, Hriday was that guy. A total filmy romantic. And today? She was sitting by the window, her face turned towards the breeze.

Tall, glowing, with a fair complexion, and the kind of jawline people get surgery for, Arohi was *the* diva of Shadley Public. And Hriday? Just a regular, confused boy with a crush and zero clue.

But today, destiny winked at him.

Arohi turned, smiled, and waved at him. *WAVED!*

"Hey Hriday, come sit with me," she said.

Hriday blinked. His brain had left the chat. For a moment, he looked as if a ghost had asked him to tea.

"Hriday? You there?" Arohi asked again.

"Yes! I mean, yes, I'll sit. Thank you. Sorry. You're cute, no, I mean… I didn't mean it like, um…" he fumbled like a true legend.

Honestly, if I weren't his best friend, I would've kicked his awkward little behind for embarrassing himself like that. Who talks like that to a cute girl?

"Are you done with the chemistry lab manual?" Arohi asked.

"Yeah! And you?"

"Almost. Need help, if you're free?"

"Free? I'd leave my own wedding for you!" Hriday nearly blurted, but quickly corrected himself, "I mean … I'm free. Happy to help."

Arohi blushed. She. Blushed.

As the bus rolled into school, the two walked into XII-B together.

Now, let me be clear, I'm Madhav, also known as Golu. Not because I'm round. Just... okay, maybe just *a little* round. Fine, 90 kgs round. But that's loveable fat, right?

I've known Hriday since we were two. We're brothers from different mothers, bonded over comics, cricket, and chole bhature. He's the Rahul to my Anjali (minus the sari scene), and I'm possessive. VERY possessive.

So obviously, I wasn't too thrilled with Arohi, the girl stealing my best friend's attention.

"Bhai!" I shouted, hugging him the moment I saw him. "I missed you so much. Don't ever leave me again!"

"Why do you make it sound like we're dating?" Hriday laughed. "Because you *are* my boyfriend, Hriday baby," I said with a wink.

"Hi, Madhav," Arohi said sweetly.

"Not interested," I said, rolling my eyes.

"Rude!" she huffed and walked away.

"Bhai, why are you like this to her?" Hriday asked, blushing like the heart-eyes emoji. "She's such a sweetheart."

"You're *mine*, Hriday. I don't share," I whispered dramatically.

"Golu, stop being weird."

"Bhai, what's in your tiffin?" I asked, my stomach growling like a lion. "Dhokla. But we're eating at break, not now."

"But they must be waiting for my mouth, Bhai! They're crying in the tiffin!"

"WE. ARE. NOT. EATING. NOW," Hriday snapped.

I sulked silently as the first-period bell rang.

Mr Dijvijay, the math teacher, entered. Tall, handsome, and serious as a heart attack. R.S. Aggarwal in hand. The blackboard read: SET THEORY.

But me? I was lost in thoughts of soft, spongy dhokla. Hriday? Lost in Arohi—her eyes, her hair, even the way she breathed seemed magical to him.

I saw Hriday stealing a glance at Arohi, completely lost in her for a second. Just then, *thwack!* A chalk flew through the air and hit him square on the forehead. It was Dijvijay Sir, who had caught him daydreaming.

"Hriday! Are you paying attention or daydreaming again?" Dijvijay Sir's voice was firm, but there was a hint of amusement in it.

Hriday blinked, snapped back to reality, and nodded sheepishly. "Sorry, Sir."

Dijvijay Sir crossed his arms and raised an eyebrow. "Alright, then. Since you're so keen on thinking about other things, let's see if you can answer this. What's the intersection of sets A and B, where A = {2, 4, 6, 8} and B = {4, 8, 10}?"

Without missing a beat, Hriday answered confidently, "The intersection is {4, 8}, Sir."

Dijvijay Sir nodded approvingly, though his gaze remained stern. "Good. Now, pay attention, Hriday. This is important. You're here to learn math, not to focus on distractions."

After the class settled, I leaned over to Hriday and whispered, "You're lucky you knew the answer, man. Otherwise, Arohi would've probably thought you were a Dumbo."

Hriday chuckled softly. "Yeah, thank god I could answer that one. But I swear, Madhav, sometimes it's hard to focus with her sitting there."

I rolled my eyes. "Dude, you need to concentrate in class, not on your crush."

Hriday nodded quickly, a sheepish grin spreading across his face. "You're right, Golu. I need to get my head in. No more distractions."

He gave a little chuckle, his gaze briefly flickering towards Arohi, but this time, he caught himself and quickly turned his attention back to the front of the class. "Focus first, crush later," he muttered, half to himself.

Lunch Break – The Turning Point

The lunch bell rang, and the hallways buzzed as students poured out of classrooms like soda fizzing out of a shaken bottle. As always, we found ourselves outside, catching up with Mohak, our third musketeer. Though he was in a different section, he practically lived in ours. That's just how things were between us.

"Chale canteen?" Mohak asked, sneaking up behind me and wrapping me in one of his dramatic bear hugs.

"Golu, take my tiffin," Hriday offered casually. "I'm staying back."

I didn't even need to ask why. Arohi was sitting right across from him, casually munching from her tiffin, completely unaware of the intense, dreamy-eyed gaze fixed on her. Hriday couldn't stop stealing glances. The way she smiled mid-bite, the soft humming she did unconsciously, it all made it seem as if she wasn't just eating lunch, she was starring in his personal rom-com.

Mohak raised an eyebrow. "Bhai, what is this behaviour? Canteen is sacred. It's our daily ritual!"

I smirked and shot Mohak a wink. "Ashiq mode's activated."

Without another word, Mohak and I exchanged devilish grins, grabbed Hriday from both sides, and *dragged* him to the canteen.

"Leave me, Bhai! Golu, yaar, leave me!" Hriday groaned, but it was already too late.

At the canteen, Mohak noticed Hriday still sneaking peeks toward the classroom windows. With a dramatic sigh, he lifted him up *again* and carried him to our usual spot near the counter.

"Shankar Bhaiya! Two plates Maggie, one samosa," Mohak declared. Our man Shankar Bhaiya, the unspoken hero of our school lunches, nodded with a smile. He loved us.

Mohak had this weird superpower of charming literally anyone. Seniors, juniors, staff, helpers, you name it. His popularity was our free pass to trouble-free adventures.

While Mohak waited for the food, Hriday, still lost in his Arohi-drenched thoughts, quietly slid his tiffin toward us. "You guys can have the dhokla."

Panic surged through me like a mini heart attack. Those dhokla were long gone. I'd eaten every last one back in class. Uh-oh.

Mohak eagerly opened the box, only to find it empty.

The silence. The slow, synchronised turn of their heads towards me. "What?" I stammered. "Why are you looking at me like that?"

"You ate them, didn't you?" Mohak narrowed his eyes.

"No! Maya Aunty must've... forgotten to pack them?" *THWACK.* Mohak landed a solid punch on my thigh. "Ouch, Bhai!" I yelped. "That hurt!"

While I rubbed my leg in agony, Hriday was still staring blankly at his Maggie, lost in a fog of emotions. Then, he finally spoke, his voice soft but unsure.

"Golu... do you think Arohi will ever be mine? Sometimes... sometimes I feel like she looks at me too. Do you think she feels the same?"

That look on his face – half hope, half doubt – hit different. Hriday, usually the confident guy who cracked jokes louder than everyone else, was now just a boy in love, vulnerable and unsure.

I paused, then placed a hand on his shoulder.

"Bhai, listen... If it's meant to be, it'll happen. Feelings don't work on a schedule. Maybe she *is* interested. But don't force anything. Be you, and let it flow."

Mohak banged the table with his spoon. "I can't believe Golu just said something sensible. Is this a fever dream?"

"Shut up," I muttered, trying to look insulted but secretly proud.

Hriday chuckled. "Fine. Switching off Majnu mode. Activating Veeru mode."

We laughed like idiots. The kind of laugh you only share when you're eighteen and the world still feels big and beautiful.

We returned to class fifteen minutes after the bell rang, without a care. It was Hindi period, after all.

Mrs Shukla, our Hindi teacher, glared at us as though we were stray cats in her temple. With her tight kurta, oversized glasses slipping down her nose, and those permanent 'Bua Ji vibes', she was terrifying in the most auntie way possible.

"Is this the time to come, you duffers?!" she barked. "OUT! And I want your grammar work tomorrow. No excuses!"

"But Ma'am," Hriday began.

"Guys, we'll figure it out," Mohak interrupted smoothly, dragging us both out with a grin.

We escaped to our secret spot, the bench behind the football ground. The forgotten corner of Shadley's. It was our haven.

Bubble gums in hand, we leaned back, taking in the moment. No pressure. No future. Just three teenage boys and the breeze, talking nonsense and dreams.

But then, just like a scene out of a movie, Arohi appeared.

She wasn't just passing by. She was walking towards us. Towards *Hriday.* With that same heart-melting smile, she walked right up to him. Hriday froze. "Hey, Hriday," she said sweetly. "Can you help me with the practicals?" Hriday blinked. It was as if he'd just touched stardust.

Mohak punched his arm to bring him back to Earth. "Hriday? You okay?" Arohi asked.

"Y-yeah. I mean… YES, yes, I'm fine," he stammered. "So… you'll help?"

"If not me, then who?" Hriday replied, this time confidently, meeting her eyes.

Arohi blushed. A little extra.

As she walked away, I muttered under my breath, "I'd still take aloo parathas over Barbie girls any day."

Mohak leaned in closer to Hriday, a knowing smile playing on his lips. "Hey, man, you've been talking about her for weeks now, and I can tell you're into her," he said, his voice low but full of excitement. "This is the perfect time. You've got this moment right now, and it won't last forever. Trust me, it's the right time to ask her out."

Hriday shifted uncomfortably, rubbing the back of his neck. "But what if she doesn't feel the same way?" he muttered, his voice tinged with doubt.

"Look, I get it," Mohak replied, shrugging casually. "But if you don't try, you'll never know. She's definitely noticing you more these days, and you're not being subtle. That's a good thing! Just go for it. Drop a few more hints, tell her how you feel... and let her see the real you."

Hriday hesitated for a moment, his mind racing with a thousand thoughts. "You really think I should do it now?"

"Absolutely," Mohak said with a grin. "This is your shot, man. Trust me, you don't want to miss it. Ask her out, show her that you care... and if she's into you too, you've got something special right there."

"Alright, I will ask her to join after her classes."

Hriday texted her, the message simple but thoughtful: "Hey Arohi, I know particles are driving you crazy. How about we meet at that quiet little café by the lake in Hauz Khas? I think I can help with your doubts, and it's a nice place to study. What do you think?"

Arohi responded almost immediately: "I could use a break, but that place sounds perfect. I'll meet you there in an hour."

An hour later, Hriday was already waiting at a small table under a canopy of green trees, the sunlight filtering through the leaves in soft, dappled patterns. The café was cozy, tucked away from the bustling city, with a peaceful atmosphere that made it feel like the rest of the world was miles away. The scent of freshly brewed coffee and the soft hum of light conversation filled the air.

Arohi walked into the café, and Hriday couldn't help but stop for a moment as he saw her. She was wearing a pair of wide blue jeans that perfectly complemented her figure, paired with a soft baby pink top that made her skin look even fairer. Her hair was left open, gently framing her face, and the Converse shoes added a casual, effortless touch to her look.

For a second, Hriday was caught off guard, his breath hitching at how effortlessly cute she looked. The way the soft pink of her top made her glow, the way her hair swayed with each step, it was like everything about her was effortlessly beautiful.

Arohi smiled when she saw him, her eyes lighting up. "Hey, Hriday!" she greeted him cheerfully, completely unaware of the effect she had on him.

She looked a little frazzled but smiled as she spotted him. "Hey," she said, sitting down across from him. "This place is amazing. I had no idea this was even here."

"I know, right?" Hriday grinned, glad to see she was at least a little less tense. "I thought it'd be a nice spot, quiet, relaxed. Perfect for particle discussions, don't you think?"

Arohi laughed softly, setting down her bag. "I'm still not sure how particles and 'perfect spots' go together, but I'm willing to find out."

Hriday chuckled. “Well, let’s dive into it. No rush, though. We’ll take our time.” He pulled out his notes, ready to help her out, but the place had a calming effect on them both. Between explanations of particle concepts and little moments of laughter, the study session became more than just an academic meeting. The peaceful ambiance allowed them to connect on a different level, and the time seemed to fly by.

As the session wound down, Hriday looked at Arohi, a small smile on his face. “You know,” he said casually, “I think you’ve got this now. You just needed a quiet spot to focus.”

Arohi nodded, feeling much more confident. “I actually do. Thanks for the help, Hriday. And for picking this place, it really made a difference.”

“Anytime,” he said, his voice soft, as he watched her relax, realising that their time together wasn’t just about particles, but something far more special.

As the study session came to an end, Arohi smiled, feeling more at ease with the topic than she had in days. She looked up at Hriday, who had been patient and thorough in explaining the tricky concepts to her. “Honestly, Hriday, I don’t know what I would’ve done without you today,” she said, her voice warm with gratitude.

Hriday gave a modest shrug, but his smile told a different story. “It wasn’t anything, Arohi. You just needed someone to break it down a little, and you did all the hard work. I’m just glad it helped.”

Arohi shook her head, her eyes sparkling with appreciation. “No, really. You made it so much easier to understand. I'd been stressing about this for days, and now... I actually feel confident about it." She paused, looking around the quiet café, the soft murmur of the surroundings adding to the peaceful moment. "And this place... it was perfect. So calming. It really helped me focus."

Hriday smiled, feeling a sense of warmth at her words. "I'm glad you liked it. It's always good to get away from the usual chaos."

Arohi's expression softened as she looked at him, a genuine smile spreading across her face. "Thanks for being patient, for taking the time to help me. I really appreciate it."

Hriday nodded, his own smile growing a little brighter. "Anytime, Arohi. Anytime."

As they gathered their things and stood up to leave, Hriday felt the sudden urge to ask Arohi something that had been on his mind. He glanced at her, his voice casual but his words soft. "So… when are we meeting next?" he asked with a small smile. "I mean, it was fun studying and all, but I was thinking it'd be nice to just chill, you know? No particles, no equations. Just... spend some time together."

Arohi blinked in surprise at his question, her cheeks suddenly flushing a soft pink. She hadn't expected it, but the simplicity and warmth in his words made her heart skip a beat. Hriday wasn't pressuring her, just asking to spend more time together, and that made it feel all the more genuine.

"Uh," she stammered, trying to hide the shy smile that was creeping up on her face. "Yeah, I'd like that. I mean, sure! That sounds really nice."

Hriday's smile widened at her instant reply, his heart doing a little happy dance at the thought of seeing her again. "Great," he said, his tone still light, but there was something a little softer behind it. "We'll figure out a time. I'll text you."

Arohi nodded, her heart racing a little as she gathered her bag. "Yeah, I'm looking forward to it."

As they walked out of the café together, a comfortable silence settled between them. Both of them knew that this time wasn't about particles or chemistry anymore, it was about something a little more exciting.

Hriday asked her if he should drop her home, but she very gracefully insisted she would escort herself as she didn't want to bother him more.

"Okay, okay, as you say, Ma'am," said Hriday.

"By the way, you... you look really good today."

Arohi's eyes widened, a slight blush creeping onto her cheeks as she tucked a strand of hair behind her ear. "Oh, thanks! I didn't think I was doing anything special today."

Hriday chuckled, feeling a bit shy but also genuinely impressed. "Trust me, it's special. You look… really cute," he said, his words simple but sincere.

Arohi blushed even deeper, her heart skipping a beat as she glanced down at her outfit, suddenly feeling a little self-conscious. "Well, I'm glad you think so."

As they walked away, neither of them could help but feel a little happier than when they had arrived. The promise of spending more time together hung in the air, and it was a thought they both cherished as they parted ways, already looking forward to the next time they'd meet. Just the TWO of them.

There's something special about meeting someone you love in a private setting, even if you see them daily. Away from the noise and distractions, you can truly connect, share a conversation, and enjoy each other's company without the pressure of others around. These quiet moments feel more genuine, allowing you to appreciate each other in a way that the usual bustle never can.

HRIDAY

My fingers hovered over the keyboard before typing.

Hriday: Hey Arohi, did you reach home safely?
Arohi: Yeah, I just got home. Thanks for checking in! ☺
Hriday: Glad to hear that! Was the ride okay?
Arohi: Yeah, it was smooth. Just a little traffic, but nothing major.
Hriday: Good to know. It's getting pretty chilly out too.
Arohi: Yeah, I noticed that! I'm all bundled up now though. 😂
Hriday: Ha-ha, smart move. 😄 Anyway, take care and relax now.
Arohi: You too, Hriday. Thanks again for today, had a great time!
Hriday: Same here, Arohi. See you tomorrow! ☺
Arohi: See you! Take care!

"Hriday, what's going on, how was your date?" Maa winked at me.

"Maa, it wasn't a date; I just went to help her out."

"Wohhh I see, and who's her by the way, what's her name?"

"Arohi." I blushed.

"And when are you making me meet her?"

"Maa, she is just a friend of mine," I stated.

"Beta, I am your Maa, and Maa knows everything. Show me her picture at least."

I showed Maa Arohi's WhatsApp display picture. It captured her radiant smile and warm personality. Her long hair cascaded softly around her shoulders, and she wore a simple light blue dress. The background featured a peaceful garden in bloom, adding a serene touch to her cheerful expression. Her eyes shone with a playful yet thoughtful gleam.

Maa gazed at Arohi's picture for a moment, then softly added, "Her eyes... they're so captivating." Maya had a strong bond with her kids, often acting more like a friend than a mother.

"Maa, I have got something cool to tell you about her," I said, smiling at my mom. "You know how I've been meaning to create a vision board? She was the one who helped me put it together," I added.

"Oh wow, that sounds nice. I thought you were going to do it yourself. How did she help?" Maa asked.

"Well, she's really talented at this kind of thing. She had so many great ideas on how to lay everything out, and she's got such a good eye for design. She made sure everything was just right."

I pointed towards the canvas by the bedside. "Look, there it is, Maa."

"Oh, that looks really good! It's so well put together. What kind of things did you put on it?" Maa asked.

"I added all my goals for the year, but Arohi made sure the colours and the design were all perfect, and that the elements were balanced. She's really into styling and beautifying things, and I think it shows here. She made sure everything had a nice flow." I smiled.

"That's lovely. It sounds like she's not just creative but also thoughtful. You're lucky to have someone like her helping you out," Maa exclaimed.

"I think I'll reach out to her the next time I need creative advice. She really knows how to make things pop."

Suddenly a message flashed on my phone which said that there were two new messages from Arohi. ♥

Arohi: [*sends a picture of the brownies*] Hey Hriday, I just baked these brownies! 😄 Do you want some tomorrow? Let me know if you're up for it!

Hriday: Oh my god, they look absolutely amazing! 😍 I can already tell they're going to taste so good! I'd love to have some tomorrow, I can't wait! You're seriously making me hungry just looking at them!

Arohi: Aww, thank you! ☺ Alright, I'll bring them for you tomorrow. Get ready for some delicious brownies!

AROHI

I've always had a soft corner for Hriday. There's something about him that makes him stand out, something every girl secretly wants. He's tall, with that effortless, messy hair that somehow always looks perfect, like he just rolled out of bed and still managed to look as if he belonged in a magazine. And his face... oh, that cute little nose that crinkles when he laughs. It's the little things, you know? And then there's his black, smart glasses which add just the right touch of sophistication that somehow makes him look even more charming. His neat look, his calm confidence – he's exactly the kind of boy I've always imagined. The kind of boy I'd want by my side.

But sometimes, I wonder if he feels the same way about me. I've caught him looking at me a few times, and my heart skipped a beat every time, but I can't help but ask myself, am I just another person in his class, or is there something more? The thought of being with him, though, makes me smile. I know I'd be the happiest girl if he ever looked at me the way I look at him. But for now, I'm left with these feelings, unsure of where they stand, unsure if they're even returned.

Walking into the kitchen, a little nervous but trying to sound casual, I said, "Pinky Didi, can you pack an extra tiffin today? I want to take along some brownies to school for Hriday." Pinky Didi was my house help and was like a second mom to me. I shared more of my life with Pinky Didi than I did with my parents as they were too occupied with the family business. Pinky Didi has loved and taken care of me since I was two.

Pinky Didi raised an eyebrow, surprised. "For Hriday? The boy you're always talking about?" She smiled teasingly while getting the tiffin box out. "Alright, let me add those brownies in, then."

"I'll make sure it's packed well. He's your classmate, right? How sweet of you!" she added

"Actually, I... I'll pack them myself. I hope he likes them," I said.

"Ahh! I see. Good luck, Arohi. I'm sure he'll love them." Pinky Didi smiled.

I then added a note in the box which said, "I only bake brownies for special ones, hope you like it Hriday ♥."

MADHAV

Every day, without fail, Arohi made sure to save the seat beside her for Hriday. It had become a quiet ritual, a moment she cherished, knowing that when he boarded the bus, he would sit next to her. As soon as she saw him climb aboard, her heart did its usual flutter, a soft warmth spreading across her cheeks. She quickly picked up her bag, making space for him to settle beside her, all the while trying to hide the growing excitement in her chest.

Hriday, as eager as always, flashed her a smile and asked for the brownies she had promised him, anticipation clear in his eyes. Arohi's heart skipped a beat at his words, but she didn't hesitate. She reached for her bag, unzipped it with a quick, practised motion, and handed him the box with a soft blush colouring her cheeks. Her hand trembled slightly as she passed it to him, the simple act of giving it to him sending a rush of emotions through her.

As Hriday opened the box, his eyes immediately caught sight of the note tucked inside. He paused, his breath catching for a moment as he read the words: *"I only bake for special ones."* Arohi held her breath, hoping he would understand the hidden meaning behind them. Her heart pounded in her chest, and she felt a sudden wave of vulnerability wash over her. But as she glanced at him, she noticed the way his gaze lingered on her, as if the note had struck a chord deep within him.

For a brief moment, everything seemed to stand still. Hriday's eyes met hers, and something unspoken passed between them. Arohi's pulse raced as she tried to keep her composure, but she couldn't ignore the way her heart beat faster in his presence. Hriday finally broke the silence, his voice soft but full of admiration as he took a bite of the brownies.

"These are amazing," he said, his praise genuine and heartfelt. "You're incredible, Arohi. I can't believe you made these just for me."

Her cheeks flushed deeper at his words, but a sense of warmth and happiness spread through her. She had always hoped he might see her for more than just the girl next to him on the bus, and in that moment, it felt like maybe… just maybe, he was starting to see her the way she saw him. The connection between them, subtle but undeniable, seemed to grow stronger, leaving both of them with the unspoken realisation that something special was beginning to take root between them.

AROHI

I had never felt anything like this before. I was happy, yet uncertain, wondering if Hriday felt the same way I did. I wanted him to be mine. Everything about him showed that he would do anything for the girl he cared about, his gestures, his kindness, the way he made everyone feel comfortable and loved. I found myself drawn to every part of him – his smile, his eyes, the way his ears and nose seemed so perfect. His voice, his lips, and the entire essence of Hriday, I was falling completely in love with him.

Lost in these thoughts, I suddenly heard a loud sound from the bus window, and before I knew it, Hriday's upper body was half leaning on me. A blue Bugatti raced past, and Hriday, completely captivated, jumped up to get a better view. His eyes widened in awe as he watched the car zip by. For a moment, I found myself wishing I could be that Bugatti, something that would capture his attention so fully. I could smell his scent, warm and sweet, like vanilla cupcakes, and for a moment, I just wanted to freeze time, to stay in that closeness forever. I won't lie, there was a part of me that wanted him to kiss him then and there. But just as quickly, he sat back down, his excitement still bubbling over as he told me how much he loved cars and bikes, just like any other boy. I was completely lost in him. Before I could catch my breath, the conductor slammed the door, signalling our arrival at school, and the moment was gone but my heart was still racing, full of thoughts of Hriday.

"Let's go Arohi." Hriday was up from the seat and was waiting for me.

Every time I looked at this boy I was completely lost in his eyelashes. Like damn man, I couldn't get such lashes after putting ten coats of mascara.

"Arohiii! Are you there?" Hriday exclaimed.

"YESS!" I said, adjusting my skirt.

Mahi was waiting for me at the main gate as usual. As soon as she saw me and Hriday getting off the bus, she playfully blew a kiss towards us. Hriday turned to me, his face filled with curiosity, and asked, "Wohhh, what was that?" I quickly shrugged it off, trying to act casual. "Nothing, she's just a crackhead," I said, trying to downplay it. I couldn't help but roll my eyes as I thought about Mahi, that bitch always managed to make me feel awkward with her antics. But at the same time, she was the only one who knew the truth about how deeply I felt for Hriday. She was the first, and only, person who understood just how much I loved him. Mahi was more like a sister to me than just a best friend. In many ways, she was the most important person in my life.

The classes went by like any other day, nothing extraordinary, except for the moments when I caught Hriday glancing my way. We exchanged shy smiles, brief but meaningful. As the bell rang for break, Hriday stepped a little closer this time and asked, "Any plans for today?" I froze. Every part of me stood still as I felt the warmth of his breath. We were so close, closer than usual, and somehow, I didn't mind at all.

"Nothing much after my tuitions," I replied, my voice barely above a whisper. He smiled, then leaned in just a little more. "So, how about we catch up?" he suggested, his eyes playful. "Without the particles and equations, of course." He winked, and I swear, my heart skipped a beat. There were butterflies not just in my stomach, but fluttering in my lungs, my heart, and some on my intestine. I couldn't help but smile, agreeing instantly, and I was pretty sure my cheeks were flushed pink by now. I don't get why my cheeks turn pink instantly, making it clear enough to anybody that I was blushing.

"Is it okay if I text you the location?" Hriday asked. "You pick the best places," I said, meeting his gaze.

He bit his lip, hiding a smile, and turned to walk towards his friends Mohak and Madhav. They both shot me a quick smile, like they knew something I didn't. I smiled back, my heart racing, then made my way to Mahi to tell her everything. "You'd better wear that red top, Aru," Mahi teased. I nodded, grinning, promising her I'd tell her every detail of what would happen next.

10 January 2021

I just lay down for a quick nap when my phone suddenly lit up with four new messages from Hriday.

Hriday: Hey beautiful! 💖
Hriday: Would it be okay if I picked you up from your tuitions at 6.30?
Hriday: I was thinking we could go to L'Opéra for some of their amazing croissants, I've been craving them!
Hriday: Plus, I owe you a treat. ♥
Arohi: Sure! I'll wait outside the classes. ☺
Arohi: But how do you owe me a treat?
Hriday: Those brownies you baked were amazing! Honestly, I could never bake anything like that or even come close. 😆
Hriday: So, I thought I'd treat you to my favourite dessert instead!
Arohi: Heheehe, you're the sweetest! ☺
Arohi: I'll wait for you, see you soon! 💕

HRIDAY

I was buzzing with excitement today, knowing it was my first proper date with the one girl I've always dreamed of spending time with. I hurried to my cupboard, eager to pick out my favourite black shirt, the one my mom had gifted me for my birthday last year from Zara.

According to her, I looked my smartest and most handsome in that shirt. I paired it with my blue-washed denim jeans and made sure my hair was styled just right to look presentable. After adjusting my specs, I added a spritz of my vanilla-scented perfume, I've always had a soft spot for sweet fragrances, and having a bit of a sweet tooth myself, it felt perfect. I rolled up the sleeves of my shirt, something Mohak once told me girls find more attractive, and slipped into my New Balance shoes.

By 6 p.m., I was ready to go. It would take me just about twenty minutes to reach Arohi's classes. I told Maa I'd be back by 9 p.m., and with a playful wink, she said, "Have fun, and there's some cash in your left pocket." I absolutely love her, she's the best. I reached the metro station, caught my train, and was at Rajiv Chowk by 6.15 p.m. After a quick five-minute walk, I arrived outside Career Compass coaching classes. With a bit of time left, I decided to pick up a bouquet of sunflowers for Arohi.

And there she was, standing, bathed in the soft golden glow of the street light, her white backpack slung casually over one shoulder. She gazed up at me, eyes shimmering with something unspoken, and my heart stuttered, as if it had forgotten how to beat in her presence. The world around us faded into a blur, and all I could see was her, Arohi. She wore a red basic strappy top, which didn't seem basic to me as Arohi made it look extraordinary, her ice-blue wide-leg denim jeans flowed effortlessly, paired perfectly with her signature black Converse, so effortlessly cool, yet so profoundly captivating.

I couldn't help but be transported back to that moment when she posted a picture in that very same top, standing outside Landour Bake House in Mussoorie, the caption echoing in my mind like a soft whisper: *"I wear red for special days."* And in that instant, a rush of realisation hit me like a wave crashing against the shore, today was no ordinary day. It was a day destined to be etched in time, a day just as special to her as it was to me.

My breath caught, as if the universe had conspired to make this moment one of a kind. It was as if time itself was holding its breath, waiting for the magic we were about to create together.

She stepped closer, her shyness radiating from her as she whispered, *"You look great, Hriday."* For a moment, I was completely lost in her presence, her beauty almost too much to process. My mind was a haze, still reeling from the sight of her. "Hriday? Are you there?" She waved her hand in front of me, pulling me back to reality.

I blinked, gathered my thoughts, and with a soft smile, I managed to say, *"Your eyes are the reason I look great, Arohi."* A delicate blush spread across her cheeks, making my heart race even faster.

Without another word, I handed her the sunflowers, their bright petals a pale reflection of the radiance she brought into my life. She took them, her smile lighting up the world around us. *"They're so pretty,"* she said, her voice soft, before adding with a playful glint in her eye, *"By the way, I love tulips. I wouldn't mind some tulips next time."*

Her words left me breathless, and before I could think, I blurted out, *"Let me buy you some then."*

But she surprised me again, her hand gently finding mine, her touch sending a warmth through me. *"Let's save something for next time,"* she said, her voice filled with sweetness and promise.

We both smiled a smile that spoke volumes and walked towards the subway, the world around us fading as we shared this quiet, perfect moment.

After a brief, quiet auto ride, we arrived at Connaught Place, where L'Opéra awaited us. The silence between us was almost palpable, both of us a little shy, hesitant to break the ice. As we stepped into the bakery, one of the staff members greeted me warmly, a bright smile lighting up her face. After all, I was a regular by then. "Quite famous, huh?" Arohi teased, giving me a playful wink. I grinned and gestured for her to follow me to a cozy corner. The cafe, with its vintage charm, felt like the perfect place for this moment, especially with the Delhi weather adding a touch of coziness, thanks to the warm space heater.

I pulled out the chair for Arohi, inviting her to sit. As she settled in front of me, I couldn't help but be captivated by the sight of her, her soft red cheeks, the gentle curve of her pink lips, everything about her felt like a dream. Just as I was lost in that moment, Arohi spoke up, breaking the spell. "So, what are we having?"

"Anything you want, I'm happy with whatever," I replied, not wanting to seem too eager.

Arohi raised an eyebrow and smiled. "This is your favourite spot. You order for me."

I nodded, giving her a warm smile. "Alright, how about a cappuccino or a latte?"

Arohi's eyes sparkled as she replied, "Cappuccino and I have been long-time lovers."

I chuckled, my heart swelling a little. "Then me and the latte are soulmates."

I called the waiter over, my voice steady as I placed our order: a cappuccino with an extra shot, just the way Arohi likes it, and a hazelnut latte with a side of Nutella and strawberry croissants to share. The waiter repeated our order, and I couldn't help but smile, knowing this moment would linger in my heart forever.

AROHI

The server arrived swiftly with our order, but my eyes were fixed on the boy sitting across from me. He was the embodiment of everything I had ever dreamed of, and in that moment, it felt like he could be mine, someday. I lifted my cappuccino with a playful wink, teasing him. "Yours looks much better though." My voice was laced with a hint of jealousy. He flashed me a knowing smile, as if he had been waiting for me to say exactly that. I took my first sip, the warmth of the coffee comforting me, but just as I did, I felt that some cream had landed on my nose.

Hriday's smile widened, and our eyes locked. I shyly returned his gaze, wiping off the cream when the world suddenly felt smaller as we shared that moment. He leaned in, his voice tender as he spoke, "I just saw the most beautiful girl I've ever laid eyes on. But don't look yet, I bet she's probably tired of people staring at her all the time. look to your left... just a little."

I turned my head slowly, my heart racing with every passing moment. "A little more..." he whispered, his eyes teasing, and I couldn't help but smile as I inched closer to the mirror. When I caught my own reflection, I couldn't hold back the laugh that bubbled up from deep inside.

I rolled my eyes in the most playful way, shaking my head. "Stop being so cute."

His expression softened, and in a voice filled with great sincerity, he said, "Arohi, I've never seen anyone more beautiful than you."

I felt the warmth of his words settle in my chest as I lowered my gaze, a shy smile forming on my lips. "Your eyes are beautiful enough to see all the beauty in me," I whispered, winking at him with a playful gleam.

And in that moment, we laughed – a sweet, innocent sound that echoed softly between us, like a melody meant just for us.

Everything felt so perfect that I wished I could freeze the moment, but sadly, I didn't have that super power. We shared our reactions to seeing each other for the first time. Hriday thought of me as a bubbly girl who gets along with everyone, but I'm actually the complete opposite – introverted and finding it hard to connect with people. To my surprise, Hriday turned out to be exactly what I had imagined – mature, grounded and sensible. As I got lost in Hriday's eyes, my phone rang. It was Pinky Didi telling me to come home because Maa and Papa were asking for me. Not once had they asked for me before, and now, just when I was with someone who made me feel alive, they wanted me. Still, I had to go – after all, they're my parents.

"I'm really sorry, Hriday, but I have to leave. Mom and Dad are home, and they want me," I said.

"Of course," he replied. "Let me just pay the bill."

"Put it on Splitwise," I joked.

"It's on you next time." Hriday winked, heading to the counter.

I felt so disappointed, wishing I could stay longer, watch him adjust his hair, lose myself in his eyes, and maybe even steal a kiss.

"Let's go, Arohi," Hriday said.

"I feel so bad for leaving so soon," I replied.

"We can catch up whenever you want," he assured me.

We both walked to the subway. "I really love spending time with you, Hriday," I told him.

He seemed a little surprised, fumbling a bit before saying, "So do I."

My metro arrived, and I waved with a smile as the doors closed between us.

HRIDAY

By this point, I had fallen even deeper for Arohi. All I could feel was love for her. She was everything I had ever imagined in the perfect girl. She embodied everything I thought a girl should be, graceful and poised, especially for someone who's just eighteen. It's rare to come across such elegance. Being around her felt like stepping into a fairytale. Her eyes were so captivating; you could get lost in them. Her nose, so delicate and sharp, caught your attention in the best way. Her lips, perfectly shaped, made you want to lose yourself in them. And that tiny mole next to her lips, just one more detail that made her even more charming. The glow on her face outshone even the brightest of actresses, I swear. She was flawless from head to toe.

At this point, I was ready to admire, adore, and spoil her. I wanted to give her the kind of treatment every girl dreams of like a princess. My thoughts were consumed by her, and I was practically losing my mind. As I was heading back to my apartment, Golu and Mohak were waiting for me. Mohak, of course, was eager to hear about what had happened, while Golu, being Golu, was just there because he wanted me to bring back some croissants for him. He snatched the paper bag out of my hand, looking like a monkey grabbing bananas from random uncles in the street.

We all sat down on the bench, and I started telling them about how everything went. And yes, before you judge me, boys talk about the smallest details with their friends too.

I started sharing the story, and I could see Mohak was really into it, while Golu was too busy devouring his Nutella croissants. But I kept going, replaying everything that happened in my mind as I told them.

"Bhai, I can tell Arohi likes you the way you like her," Mohak said.

"How can you tell?" Golu asked, raising an eyebrow.

"Man, she didn't want to leave Hriday. She wanted to stay longer. That says a lot, don't you think?" Mohak replied.

"What if she just enjoys being around Hriday, just like I do?" Golu teased, winking.

"Golu, you won't understand," Mohak replied, frustrated.

"Yeah, yeah, I know I can never win against this love guru," Golu said, rolling his eyes, taking another big bite of his third croissant.

"Anyway, whatever it is, I'm falling even harder for her, and I can't wait to see her tomorrow," I said, standing up and heading towards the gate.

"Bhai, your block is behind! Where are you going?" Golu called out.

"Arohi likes tulips. I'm going to get some so I can give them to her tomorrow," I shouted back. "Tell Maa I'll be back in twenty minutes!"

AROHI

There were tulips on my bench, and I noticed Mahi staring at them, utterly clueless. A soft smile crossed my face as I watched her, and I couldn't help but say something. "This boy, how far can someone go to make me happy?" I said, my voice soft, but my eyes betraying me, becoming misty with emotion. Mahi immediately caught the change in my gaze and asked, "Hriday?"

I shyly nodded, my heart skipping a beat, and whispered, "Who else?"

With a mischievous wink, she wrapped an arm around me in a warm side hug. But then, her curiosity took over. "But where is he?" she asked.

I looked at Mahi, and she quickly began searching the class, her eyes scanning for any sign of Hriday. Finally, she spotted Madhav and asked him, "Have you seen Hriday?"

Madhav's face softened, his tone laced with sadness. "Hriday and Mohak are at basketball practice. They've got their final match with St. Xavier's tomorrow, so they won't be joining us for class today."

I could tell by the way Madhav spoke that he was missing his friends, and I felt a gentle pang in my heart. Without wasting a second, I grabbed Mahi's hand and pulled her out of the classroom.

"Where are we going?" Mahi asked, struggling to keep up with my pace.

"Faster, Mahi," I urged, a sudden surge of excitement filling me. "Towards the basketball court. I need to thank Hriday."

In no time, we reached the court. And there he was, Hriday, drenched in sweat, wearing his shorts and jersey, completely lost in the game. Every move he made was filled with such focus and energy, effortlessly sinking shots into the hoop. In that moment, I swear he looked like the most handsome guy on Earth. Who wouldn't fall for a tall, dark, and handsome boy, playing basketball with so much intensity?

Mahi, ever the enthusiastic one, waved her hands and jumped to catch his attention, and when Hriday saw us, he smiled at me, his gaze warm and knowing. He gestured for me to wait as he finished the match. I flashed him a thumbs-up, completely captivated by him. I couldn't take my eyes off him, even when someone else made a basket, a small part of me felt a little irritated, wishing it had been him. My gaze remained glued to Hriday, not once blinking as I watched him run with the ball, his movements graceful yet powerful.

The match ended after what felt like no time at all. As he wiped the sweat from his face with a towel, sipping water from his bottle, I wished I could freeze that moment forever, lost in the sheer allure of him.

Then, just as I was completely immersed in the charm of the boy in front of me, he looked up and, in an instant, he was standing before me, his presence filling the space.

"Hello, girls... what brings you here?" Hriday asked with a curious smile.

"Madhav said we'd find you at the court," Mahi replied softly.

Hriday looked at us with that familiar charm and said,

"So, since you've found me, mind telling me what brings you here?"

I stood there, lost in the moment, words caught somewhere between my heart and lips.

Mahi nudged me gently with her elbow, urging me to speak. Finally, I managed to say, "Hriday... could we meet after class, if you're free? Only if it's possible."

He smiled, eyes glinting mischievously. "For you, I'll make *everything* possible," he said, his tone light yet laced with a quiet intensity.

Everyone around could tell, I was blushing deep pink, completely exposed with my emotions.

"This time, *I* choose the place," I added, gathering my courage as I turned to leave for class.

Hriday grinned, then winked with a playful murmur, "As you wish... Ma'am."

HRIDAY

After a long, exhausting day at the court, I finally made it back home. I was tired to the bone, yet there was a certain thrill that lingered, the kind that comes from knowing you got to skip classes, scored full attendance, and had no assignments waiting. A small, cheeky win.

But amidst it all, something was missing, or rather, someone. I missed being with Golu and, most of all, adoring Arohi. The thought of meeting her later today made everything feel lighter. I quickly dialled Golu, filled him in on my day, and shared what the evening held for me. It struck me that I hadn't spent time with golu in quite a while either. I told Golu that once my match wraps up tomorrow, I'm all his. No delays. No distractions.

Just as we ended the call, an irresistible aroma wrapped itself around me, biryani. My heart leaped. Maa stood there with a steaming plate, her smile warmer than the dish itself. My all-time favourite. I rushed towards the dining table, but Maa, being Maa, ordered me to go freshen up first. If only she knew, biryani doesn't wait for anyone; we wait for it. Still, I complied, slipping into my most comfortable boxers and an old tee, and hurried back.

One bite in and I was in heaven. Maa had outdone herself, each grain was infused with flavour, love and comfort. I was completely lost in it when my phone buzzed. A notification lit up the screen: "2 new messages from Arohi ♥".

"Are you tired? Should we postpone it?"

My heart skipped a beat. *This girl… cares. About me?* Without a second thought, and with biryani-flavoured fingers, I replied: "*Not at all! I'm all up.*"

"*I'll be waiting for you at Central Secretariat subway by 5. We're going to Humayun's Tomb, and then Khan Market, to pick up my dress,*" messaged Arohi.

"*Sounds great. I'll be there on time, ma'am,*" I sent back, grinning.

She replied with a simple smiley. And just then, Maa's voice rang out again, playful and sharp: "Who is more important to you than biryani?"

I smiled, cheeks turning a soft shade of pink, and lovingly returned to the plate, heart full and stomach ready.

After a short nap, it was time to get ready. I hurried to switch on the geyser, craving a warm, refreshing bath.

"Maa, can you please iron my white shirt?" I called out.

"Where are you off to?" Maa shouted from the hall.

"Nothing much, just meeting some friends," I replied casually.

"Friends or *special* friends?" she teased, her voice echoing with mischief.

"Just friends, Maa!" I called back, trying to sound casual, though I couldn't help but smile. For some reason, I always felt the need to look my absolute best in front of Arohi.

I chose my crisp white shirt and paired it with the lightest shade of blue jeans I owned. It was already five o'clock. I quickly brushed my hair, put on my black-rimmed glasses, sprayed a hint of my favourite chocolaty perfume, and slid into my Nikes.

"Will you have dinner with us or with your friends?" Maa asked with a knowing smile and a little wink.

"With you guys, of course! Bye Maa, I'm running late!"

"Oh no, my watch!" I gasped. "Maa, can you please bring me my silver watch?" I called out in a rush.

"Hriday and his watches, inseparable duo!" she teased. "What made you forget it today?"

I laughed. "Oh Maa, you're so dramatic!"

With my watch finally on my wrist, I dashed out and headed to the subway. I caught the metro to Central Secretariat, just as Arohi had asked.

Soon, the announcement came: "Next stop is Central Secretariat. Doors will open on the right."

Without wasting a moment, I texted Arohi, "*Hey! I'm here*," along with a quick selfie that showed the platform number.

"Just 2 more minutes, I'll be there," she texted back.

There she was… and in that moment, my heart forgot how to beat. She chose the stairs over the escalator and with every step she took towards me, the world around her faded into a blur. It was as if the universe had dimmed its lights so only she could shine.

Her hair danced with the breeze as if it too was celebrating her arrival. She wore a white chikankari kurti with matching pants – an outfit that didn't just suit her, it was made for her. The tiniest jhumkas adorned her ears, swinging gently, and a single black bindi graced her forehead like the final stroke of a masterpiece.

Her juttis completed the vision, white with delicate red and yellow threadwork, each thread seemed to tell a story of its own. And to me, it was all happening in slow motion, the girl I love, walking to me like a scene from the most beautiful dream I never wanted to wake up from.

And then… she was in front of me, waving, smiling, glowing. I stood there frozen, overwhelmed by her presence. Somehow, I found my voice and whispered, "How could someone look so perfect?" Her cheeks, already pink, blushed deeper, and her eyes sparkled like stars answering my question without a word.

She gently tugged my hand, pulling me towards the metro.

"We need to head to Khan Market," she said with a spark in her eyes.

"Where are we going first, Arohi?" I asked, slightly out of breath.

"To pick up my jersey," she replied casually.

Jersey? My eyebrows shot up in surprise.

"Wait, what? You're an athlete? How did I not know this?"

She laughed, rolling her eyes. “No, you idiot. It’s not like that. Just stay calm.”

There was a rush in her step, something urgent in the air, and I had no idea what was going on.

We walked through the buzzing lanes of Khan Market until she stopped in front of a cozy little store with a sign that read “Custom Creation Studio”.

“Let’s go!” she said, her voice dancing with excitement.

“But… why a customisation store?” I asked, rubbing my head, still lost in her little mystery.

“Just follow me, Hriday,” she said with a playful command in her voice, and I did, like I always would.

Inside, she walked straight up to the front desk.

“Hi, I’m Arohi. I think I spoke to someone earlier, I ordered a customised Lakers jersey.”

The woman behind the counter smiled. “Yes, ma’am. It’s ready.”

A Lakers jersey?

I blinked in disbelief. “Arohi, what are you up to?”

She smirked. “Just wait, Hriday… you’ll see.”

Moments later, the employee returned with a bright yellow Lakers jersey in hand. Arohi’s face lit up with the widest, most radiant smile.

“Please check it once,” the woman said as she handed it over.

Arohi slowly unfolded the jersey. My eyes locked on the number **23** and the name **LeBron James** stitched proudly across the back.

In that instant, my heart leaped. I grabbed her by the shoulders, turning her to face me, my hands trembling with excitement.

"What did you do?" I asked, shaking her gently.

And then, in the softest, most loving voice, she said, "Hriday… I know how much you love LeBron. And it's your match tomorrow, I'm going to be there, cheering for you. I'll be wearing this."

Something in me melted.

LeBron wasn't just a player, he was *the* reason I fell in love with basketball. And this girl… this incredible girl thought of something so thoughtful, just to bring a smile to my face.

Without thinking, I pulled her into the tightest hug, overwhelmed by emotion. Then it hit me, I might've held her a little too long. I slowly pulled away, awkwardly apologising. "I-I'm sorry… it was just out of excitement."

But before the apology could fully leave my lips, she looked up at me with a bold glint in her eyes and said, "Was it *just* excitement?" A pause.

Then, with a smirk, she said, "Nonetheless… I liked it."

The employee handed us the packed jersey, but my heart was already full.

And just like that, we stepped out of the store, not just with a jersey, but with a moment I'd never forget.

We took a quick auto ride to Humayun's Tomb. "Arohi, can I ask you something?" I said.

"Go ahead," she replied with a gentle smile.

"Why this place?" I asked, curious.

"I don't know… there's this one spot here. It's kind of hidden, unexplored," she said softly. "But it feels calming amidst all the chaos. I often come here to paint… or to journal."

"All by yourself?" I asked.

"Yes," she smiled, "and you're the first person I've ever brought here." She winked.

"Oh! Then I must be the lucky one," I said, playfully returning the wink.

"You never know," she replied, teasingly.

I got in line to collect the entry tokens, while Arohi led me to a secluded part of the monument. Just a few girls were around, making reels or taking pictures. It was a quiet, dome-like structure, with a view of the lush gardens. A tall tree stood ahead of us, silhouetted against the warm hues of the setting sun. Birds were returning to their nests, and a cool breeze began to wrap around us.

We sat, a little closer than before.

"This is… perfect. It feels like a scene out of a movie," I said.

"See? I have a good eye for spots." She smiled.

"No doubt about that." I laughed softly. "So?" I asked.

"So?" she echoed, raising an eyebrow. "You want me to say something?" I smiled.

"Yes… I mean, only if you want to," she said, her voice suddenly softer.

"I've been to this place so many times," she continued, looking ahead, "but today it feels different. Hriday… there's something about being with you that feels special. Like I don't have to try. I don't have to fill every silence with words. I'm just... happy. Even the quiet feels beautiful."

I sat there, frozen, not because of the evening chill, but because of her words. Arohi had just said something that completely disarmed me. My heart was racing, but in the stillness of that moment, everything felt just right.

I've always been the worst when it comes to expressing how I feel, and true to form, when Arohi shared something so heartfelt, all I managed to say was... "Okay."

Seriously. *Okay.*

Who says *okay* in a moment like that?

She didn't say anything after that. Just went quiet, letting her eyes wander across the beauty of the place. But while she admired the view... I couldn't take my eyes off her.

Arohi, she was the only girl I'd ever adored this much since Maa. And in that quiet moment, I whispered to myself, *"If it's her today, it'll be her till the end."*

Hriday, just say it. Say what you feel, my mind screamed.

But being the absolute dumbass that I am, I dodged it all... and started talking about the most random things.

Honestly, if Mohak had been there, he would've smacked me back to my senses.

Hours passed. Somehow, in between laughter and stories, we ended up sharing everything under the sky. I was loving every second of it, every word, every silence.

And then, after a long pause, she broke the rhythm. "It's time for me to leave," she said.

I stayed quiet. Not a single hint from me... not even a whisper of how much I wanted her to stay.

"Hriday… do you want me to stay?" she asked softly.

"I mean… just a bit," I said, trying not to sound too desperate.

She smiled faintly, looking away.

"Even I don't want to leave. If I could, I'd stay here forever," she whispered, her voice so low it barely reached me, but it hit like a storm.

My jaw dropped.

And there I was again, quiet. Frozen. A complete idiot.

"Do you want to say something, Hriday?" she asked. "Or should I leave?" Her voice trembled. Just a little. But enough for my heart to break open.

"Yes! I want to… But..." I said.

"But…?" she tilted her head, her eyes searching mine.

I closed my eyes, took a breath so deep I thought it would shatter me. And then I opened them, looked straight into hers, and said, "Arohi… I LIKE YOU."

She didn't blink. Just stared into me. Her cheeks slowly turned the softest shade of pink, and I swear the sky blushed with her.

She smiled, the kind of smile that lingers in your dreams.

"I like you too," she said. "But why didn't you tell me earlier?"

"I don't know… I kept wondering, *was it the right time? What if you stopped talking to me?* So many stupid questions held me back."

She laughed, gently. "If you hadn't confessed today, I might've stopped talking to *you*!"

"You… really mean it? You like me too?" I asked, still half in disbelief.

"Yes, Hriday," she said, this time with all the clarity in the world, "I've always wanted to be with you."

And in that moment, beneath the fading sun, with the hush of the evening wind swirling around us, I realised something.

Sometimes, love doesn't need a grand gesture.

Sometimes, all it takes is one trembling voice, one brave sentence, and a silence that finally speaks everything.

AROHI

Everything seemed to pause the moment Hriday confessed his feelings. The evening slipped quietly into night, yet I remained frozen in disbelief. The boy I had secretly longed to call mine… was finally mine.

I turned to steal a glance at him, he was gazing up at the stars, lost in thought. "Hriday, what's going on in that head of yours?" I asked softly.

"Nothing," he said, his voice warm and thoughtful. "Just wondering how I'm going to keep *MY GIRL* the happiest. I'm a responsible man now, after all."

Those two words, *MY GIRL*, wrapped around my heart like a lullaby. Tears of joy welled up in my eyes.

"You don't even realise how happy you've made me, Hriday," I whispered. "Just being near you makes me feel loved, safe… complete."

He turned to me then, his eyes darker and deeper than the night sky. "Arohi," he began, his voice slightly trembling, "I know it's early… but I want this, *us*, forever. I don't want a fleeting romance. It's forever or nothing."

I smiled through the tears. "We might be young, Hriday, but I'm yours. I want to live it all with you, every ordinary moment, every adventure. And I'm not going anywhere… not without you, BABYYY."

His laughter broke through the seriousness, soft and boyish. "Did you just call me *baby*?" he teased, eyes wide with mock shock. "Already? Oh no, I might die."

I giggled. "Okay okay, maybe too soon?"

"No," he said, stepping closer, so close I could hear the rhythm of his heart, steady and strong. "I want to be called that. Especially if it's by you."

Just as I wished time would freeze around us, the spell was broken by the sharp *crack* of a stick tapping against the pathway. The distant sound of a whistle followed, growing closer. We turned to see the watchman making his rounds, tapping the ground rhythmically and calling out for everyone to clear the area, it was time to close the gates.

Hriday stood up the moment the watchman's voice echoed, and without a word, extended his hand towards me. I took it instinctively, rising to my feet, feeling the ease of our connection in that simple gesture. We began walking towards the gate, the evening air growing colder with every step. I shivered slightly, realising I had forgotten my cardigan in the rush to meet him.

Almost reading my mind, Hriday turned to me with concern etched on his face. "Arohi, why didn't you bring a sweater?"

I smiled sheepishly. "It didn't match my kurti... and honestly, I was in such a hurry to see you, I completely forgot my cardigan."

He chuckled, his eyes softening. "Aww, my poor baby... I swear, one day I'm going to die from how adorable that face is."

He immediately offered his jacket. "Wear this."

But I shook my head with a grin. "Aesthetics matter."

That made him burst into laughter. "Girls… just being girls," he said, shaking his head in disbelief.

We were just a short distance from the gate when we noticed an elderly woman sitting quietly by the pathway, surrounded by handwoven shawls displayed neatly beside her. Her presence had a quiet grace, almost as though time had slowed around her.

Hriday paused and looked at me, his eyes twinkling with mischief and care. "Think any of these would go with your aesthetics?" he teased gently. "And will you actually wear them?"

I nodded, curious and charmed by the moment. We walked up to her stall. She looked up with a smile that held stories of years gone by, clearly surprised and pleased that someone had stopped.

"These shawls are so beautiful, Aunty," Hriday said warmly.

"Thank you, Beta," she replied, her voice gentle and trembling. "I made them all myself."

Hriday scanned the collection thoughtfully. "Do you have anything in white? It'll match her perfectly." He glanced at me as he said it, and my heart fluttered.

"Yes, yes, Beta, I have three in white. Please take a look." She opened a small bundle and revealed them with care.

They were all exquisite, each one with a delicate story woven into its threads. My eyes lingered on one in particular, soft, elegant and timeless. But I said nothing, silently hoping Hriday would choose it.

He turned to me. "Which one do you like?"

I smiled and shrugged. "Whichever you pick is perfect for me."

He considered them for a moment, then reached out and picked the very shawl I had fallen in love with. As he handed it to me, I couldn't hide my excitement. "I loved this one too!" I said, almost breathless with joy.

Hriday's eyes lit up. "I'm already loving this phase," he whispered, watching me as if I was the only thing in the world.

He turned back to the old woman and picked another shawl, admiring its weave. "How much for both, Aunty?"

Before answering, she folded her hands slightly and smiled with teary eyes. "Thank you, Beta. No one even stops by here… people think these shawls aren't worth much. But each one takes days, sometimes weeks, to weave. It's all handmade."

"I know the kind of love and effort that goes into something made by hand," Hriday said softly.

She hesitated. "1,500 for both, Beta."

Hriday handed her two thousand rupees without blinking. "Please keep it, Aunty. Think of it as a little token from your son."

Her hands trembled. "Beta… this is too much…"

Hriday smiled gently, then unwrapped the shawl he had chosen for himself and softly draped it over her shoulders. "This one is for you, Aunty."

Tears welled up in her eyes as she looked at him, completely moved. "You didn't need to do all this…"

"But I wanted to. Accept it from your son," he said, kneeling briefly and holding her hand with such kindness that even the stars might have paused to watch.

I had often heard our batchmates speak of Hriday, how kind, caring, and effortlessly genuine he was with everyone around him. But today, I wasn't just hearing about it… I was witnessing it with my own eyes, feeling it with my heart.

He returned to me, unfolding my new white shawl. "May I?" he asked.

I nodded, and he gently wrapped it around me. The warmth of the fabric was nothing compared to the warmth of the gesture. I felt safe. I felt loved. I felt *his*.

From behind us, we heard the aunty's tender voice, "Beta, you're too pretty for this shawl."

I smiled and thanked her softly.

Hriday looked back at her and said with quiet pride, "Aunty, anything she wears becomes even more beautiful."

And just like that, we walked away, wrapped not just in wool, but in something far deeper – care, sincerity, and a love that was already beginning to feel like forever.

"What's next on the itinerary, my girl?" Hriday asked, his voice laced with playful curiosity.

I felt my cheeks flush with the warmth of his gaze.

"Let's head out for some momo," I said, smiling. "I'm seriously craving them."

He chuckled. "In a city like Delhi, that's the toughest craving to satisfy, we're spoiled with choices! Where do we even begin?"

Without hesitation, I whispered, "Majnu ka Tilla. They serve some of the finest momos and the dreamiest laphing you'll ever taste."

His eyes lit up instantly. "It's Friday night, the vibe there might be magical," he said, already pulling out his phone. Moments later, a cab was on its way, as if summoned by fate itself.

As the city lights blurred past us, Hriday turned to me and began to talk, not just about places or food, but about his heart. He spoke of how his parents met, how they still laughed like newlyweds and held hands like they had just fallen in love. His father, a dignified officer at the Parliament. His mother, a warrior of kindness, working with an NGO to help people break free from addiction. His brother, lost in books and dreams at MICA, chasing an MBA in Ahmedabad.

I didn't speak much. I didn't have stories as weighty or grand. But I listened, every word of his story became a page I wanted to read forever.

Soon, twenty minutes passed like a soft breeze, and suddenly, we were standing at the entrance of Majnu ka Tilla, the night buzzing around us like a heartbeat.

"I know a stall," I said, grinning, "that serves the best paneer momos and the kind of laphing that could change your life."

Hriday nodded, ready to follow, but he vanished from my side for a moment. I turned, and there he was: standing by a modest florist, gently selecting a bouquet of tulips, as if choosing stars from the night sky.

"Hriday, you don't have to,"

His fingers found my lips before I could finish what I was saying. "Arohi," he whispered, "never stop me from doing something for you. Ever."

And just like that, with tulips in my hands and his words echoing in my heart, I fell a little deeper into whatever this was – this beautiful, slow-burning story we were writing.

Within no time, we had arrived at the little momo stall tucked away like a secret in the heart of Majnu ka Tilla. Lanterns swayed gently overhead, and the aroma of sizzling fillings and steamed dough curled through the air like a promise. The momos? Divine. The chutney? Spicy perfection.

But his presence, that warmth beside me, that softness in his eyes, was the flavour I'd never forget.

Just as we finished our third plate of momos, our bellies full and hearts light, we decided to wander through the quiet lanes, letting the night pull us forward like a slow, sweet melody. To our surprise, the usually buzzing streets of Majnu ka Tilla were still, silent, as though the world had paused just for us. The breeze whispered between prayer flags, and faint chimes echoed in the distance.

As we strolled, Hriday spotted a narrow flight of stairs winding upwards towards a tiny tattoo studio, now shuttered for the night. A soft grin curved his lips.

"Can we sit up there for a bit?" he asked, his voice lower now, as if not to disturb the hush around us.

I nodded without a thought, drawn to the softness in his eyes. We climbed a few steps and settled into the worn concrete, tucked between dreamcatchers in shop windows and strings of faded Tibetan flags fluttering gently above us, like pieces of sky stitched in colour.

From that little perch, the world felt far away. The city, the noise, even time itself, it all seemed to dissolve. Hriday turned towards me slowly, and without a word, his hand came to rest on my knee. My heart leaped, loud and fast and completely unashamed. I was sure he could hear it.

Then, with the gentleness of a secret being told for the very first time, he spoke. "Arohi… you're the first person I've ever wanted to call mine. And I want you to be the last."

I looked into his eyes, deep, unguarded, glowing like they held constellations just for me.

"I've never felt this," he continued, his thumb brushing softly across my leg, "not with anyone. But with you… it's like everything makes sense. It's scary, and beautiful. And I don't want it to end."

His words curled into my chest and stayed there.

"Hriday," I whispered, my voice trembling with everything I felt, "I've fallen so hard for you… and I don't know how to imagine anything without you in it."

We sat there, lost in confessions and soft laughter, our hearts unfolding like petals in moonlight. Eventually, the night began to stretch and tug at us, hinting it was time to leave. I turned to him with a voice heavier than I meant. "Should we call it a day?"

He looked at me, not with an answer, but with a question of his own. He leaned in, closer than before, close enough for the strands of his hair to brush mine like a whisper. "Can we stay a little longer?"

My breath caught. "For how long?" I asked, my nose grazing his now, the space between us no longer real.

He didn't hesitate.

"Forever," he breathed.

And in that moment, the world disappeared. Our lips met, soft at first, then all at once, it started slow, tender, searching, like a question neither of us wanted to end. But then he deepened it, his hand rising to cradle my jaw as if he was afraid I'd disappear. My fingers curled into his shirt, pulling him closer. His lips moved against mine with aching urgency, soft, but claiming, as though he'd waited a lifetime for this moment.

The kiss was fire and moonlight, breathless pauses and soft gasps, his thumb tracing circles on my thigh, my hand tangled in his hair. The world melted away. Nothing else existed but the warmth of his mouth, the pressure of his body leaning into mine, the taste of something sweet and dangerous and completely ours.

And when we finally parted, our foreheads resting against each other, eyes still closed… I knew. I had crossed into a feeling I'd never come back from.

It was no longer just the night we were in, it was a feeling, a forever, that began with us.

HRIDAY

I couldn't quite grasp what had just happened, it was so much more than just a kiss. As we gently pulled away, I still felt the softness of her lips lingering on mine. Her eyes remained closed, her breath coming quicker than before, and her cheeks had turned a shade deeper than the pink of her kurti.

"Arohi, are you okay?" I asked softly.

She slowly opened her eyes and looked straight into mine. And in that moment… it was magic. Time stood still. That look, tender, vulnerable, full of wonder, made me understand what love *truly* feels like. It wasn't just about affection; it was about being seen, being held, being cherished.

Tears welled up in her eyes, glimmering like stardust. I cupped her face gently, pressing a soft kiss to her cheek.

"I am, and always will be, the one who celebrates you, Arohi," I whispered, my voice trembling with emotion.

Before I could finish my sentence, she wrapped her arms tightly around me, burying her face into my chest. I could feel her trembling, her quiet sobs echoing into my heartbeat.

"I've never known what love feels like," she murmured. "Mom and Dad… they don't see me. For them, everything is just business and money. They've forgotten I exist. I've longed for a moment like this… someone to just hold me. And now… I feel so light, Hriday. With you, I finally feel… loved."

I gently pulled her back to look into her eyes, brushing a strand of hair from her face.

"Arohi, no matter what comes, I will always love you, in every way, in every form, endlessly."

She nodded through her tears, then asked with a quiet, hopeful voice, "Can I… hug you once more, before we leave?"

This time, I held her tighter, like I never wanted to let go. I could feel her tears soak into the back of my shirt, warm and real. I slowly pulled away, kissed her forehead tenderly, and offered to drop her home.

I booked a cab to New Friends Colony, the upscale Delhi neighbourhood where Arohi lived, known for its opulent bungalows and high-profile residents. Within seconds, the cab arrived.

"OTP, Sir?" the driver asked.

"3478," I replied, my gaze drifting back to Arohi.

She stepped into the cab, still clutching the jersey and next to it, the tulips I had brought for her. Her expression hadn't changed. She was still in awe, still dazed by the whirlwind of emotions that had just swept through both of us.

And so was I.

She buried her face into me, choosing silence over words. I held her gently, but inside, my heart was aching. I couldn't understand how someone could ever fail to cherish a soul like Arohi. How long had she been living like this, quietly carrying the weight of being unseen, unloved?

The thought of it broke something inside me. It felt unjust… deeply, cruelly unfair.

Still holding her, I slowly reached for her hand. She looked up at me, and for the first time in that moment, a fragile smile flickered across her lips, like a sunrise peeking through the cracks of a long, stormy night.

And then, in the softest voice I'd ever heard, she whispered, "Everything I love eventually leaves me. I just… I just hope you stay."

I looked into her eyes, eyes that had endured more than they should've ever had to.

"Arohi," I said, my voice barely above a whisper, "if pain couldn't break you, if silence couldn't silence your light… then I promise, with every heartbeat in me, I'll never be the one who walks away. I won't just stay; I'll stand by you even when the world forgets how to."

She didn't say anything after that, she didn't need to. Her eyes said it all, as they filled once again with tears, not of sadness this time, but of finally being seen, and finally being held for who she truly was.

And in that moment, I knew: I wasn't just holding her hand. I was holding her trust, her fears, her past… and her hope.

Soon we entered the lanes of New Friends Colony and I could see Arohi's face change into something I hadn't seen before. She became sort of bothered and there was a discomfort that I could feel and sense. I could hear "turn right and you will be at your destination" through the cab driver's phone, as I checked out his phone's screen I could see "two minutes until we reach the destination" and Arohi was so quiet that I could hear her breathe.

As we turned into the lanes of New Friends Colony, I noticed a shift in Arohi. Her face, usually so composed, clouded over with something unfamiliar, an unease that wrapped around her like a sudden chill. I could feel it in the air between us, heavy and silent.

From the cab driver's phone came a calm voice, "*In 200 metres, turn right. Your destination is ahead.*" As expected from Google Maps, it was emotionless and precise. I glanced at the screen, just two minutes left. Two minutes, yet Arohi hadn't said a word. Something was stirring beneath her silence, and I couldn't look away.

"Arohi… are we there yet?" I asked softly, sensing the shift in her mood.

She didn't respond with words, just a faint "hmm..." That one sound, or rather the silence that followed, confirmed what I had been feeling for a while now: something was bothering her. I turned towards her, concern edging into my voice.

"What's wrong, Arohi? You've been so quiet… especially after such an amazing day."

She looked at me then, really looked. There was an intensity in her eyes, a flicker of something she was trying to hide. It was as if she wanted to say something, but the weight of it kept her silent.

Before I could ask any more questions, the car rolled to a stop and the driver turned back. "Sir, we're here."

I glanced out the window, and my eyes widened. A grand iron gate stood before us, crowned with a nameplate that read "Khanna Mansion". It was bigger than anything I'd seen before, definitely more imposing than the main gate of my own society.

My eyes scanned the scene in a second: four or five cars were lined up neatly outside. One of them was unmistakably a BMW, and the other, a fiery red G-Wagon. The rest were hidden in the shadows or behind the massive trees that framed the entrance. I couldn't see the mansion clearly, but the glimpse I got through the lush, manicured trees told me everything, it was huge. Grand. Bigger than any celebrity home I'd only seen on screens.

And this… this was her house.

I turned to her, eyes wide with surprise.

"Arohi… you guys have a G-Wagon?" I asked, unable to hide my excitement. She simply nodded, murmuring another quiet "hmm".

Before I could process her silence further, a security guard strode towards our cab, annoyance etched on his face.

"Hey, move your vehicle! What do you think this place is for?"

But then he saw her.

His tone shifted instantly. "Oh… Aaruu Didi!" Arohi stepped out of the car, nodding slightly at him.

I reached for the door handle to get out too, but before I could, she turned to me quickly.

"Don't get out," she said gently. "It's late… just head home. I'll see you tomorrow. At your basketball match, okay?"

I paused, surprised by the sudden distance in her voice.

"Okay, Arohi," I said, leaning forward, hoping to end the night with a kiss.

But she pulled back, avoiding my eyes.

Instead, she waved a soft goodbye and walked off toward the mansion.

I stayed there in the cab, watching her until she disappeared behind those giant gates. Not once did she look back.

There was a strange heaviness in my chest. Something about the way she left, quiet, distant, unreadable, felt… off. But I held on to hope. I knew Arohi. And whatever it was, she would tell me. Eventually.

I had just stepped into the house when my phone buzzed. It was Golu.

"Bro! We're still meeting, right? Who's coming to whom?"

I sighed, exhaustion pulling at every part of me.

"Bhai… I'm sorry. Can we meet tomorrow instead? I'm just really tired tonight."

He paused, his voice changing tone.

"What's wrong, bro? You sound… heavy. Is everything okay?"

"I'm fine, Golu. Really. Just… meet me at the match tomorrow, okay?" I tried to keep my voice even.

There was silence on the other end for a beat longer than usual before he said a quiet, "Okay."

And then the call ended.

I knew he'd been waiting for me the entire day. And I hated disappointing him. But something about Arohi's behaviour today had left a strange weight on my chest. I didn't have the energy to be around anyone just now.

A soft beep pulled me from my thoughts.

I had one new message from Arohi. ♥

Arohi: Are you home?

Hriday: Yes!

Arohi: Listen Hriday, I'm sorry… for what happened today.

Hriday: It's okay. I figured something real might be going on.

Arohi: Hm.

Hriday: If you want to talk… I'm here. Whenever you're ready.

Arohi: Tomorrow, after your match. Can we?

Hriday: Okay!!

Arohi: Also, you owe me a treat. I *know* you guys are going to win.

Hriday: 😄😄

Her last message brought a calm I hadn't felt all day. Just knowing she was still there, soft, teasing, gave me peace. It was enough to silence my doubts, even if only for a moment.

My thoughts wandered, unbidden, to the way her lips had felt against mine. That kiss… our first. It played in my mind in slow motion. My heart raced as I closed my eyes, still able to feel her breath, the softness of that stolen moment. Goosebumps traced my arms.

"Hridayyyyy!!"

Maa's voice cut through the quiet like a sudden breeze through a curtain.

"Yes, Maa!" I called out, snapping back to reality and running to her, wrapping my arms around her from behind.

"Help me set the table, beta. And call your papa, we're having dinner."

"Maa, I… don't feel like eating. I want to keep it light tonight. Finals are tomorrow."

She turned to me, a mix of concern and affection in her eyes.

"It's not good to sleep on an empty stomach, Beta."

"I had some momos earlier," I murmured, "just give me a glass of milk before you sleep? That'll be enough."

"Okay. Let me know when," she said, brushing my arm gently. Her eyes said the rest, she understood.

She signed for me to go rest. I nodded and turned away.

But even as I walked back to my room, my mind was already with her. With Arohi.

25 February 2021 – Shadley vs. Xavier's

HRIDAY

The court felt electric.

The thump of sneakers echoed through the court as we warmed up, our jerseys already clinging to us from the adrenaline. As captain of Shadley's, I rallied my boys, shouting over the rising buzz of the crowd.

"Let's lock this down, boys. Heads high, hearts on fire."

And then came Mohak, loud, fearless, voice cutting through the noise.

"Captain, we're winning today, no matter how, no matter what!"

We broke out in a chorus of roars, the kind that vibrated in the ribs. Fists in the air, palms colliding, and then we scattered to our marks. I felt the weight of the moment settle in my chest like iron, but then, I saw her.

Arohi.

She entered the hall with Mahi beside her, and just like that, time bent. The game, the crowd, even my own pulse blurred. She was glowing.

She wore the jersey like it belonged to the moment, paired effortlessly with a blue denim skirt, falling just enough to tease without trying. Her white Nike sneakers bore that familiar green swoosh, and that high ponytail. God, it made her look like every sports fantasy ever dreamed up under stadium lights.

She waved.

I don't even remember waving back, I was too busy giving her the best damn smile I've ever smiled. Her lips shaped two perfect words.

"All the best," mine replied, just as softly.

"Thank you."

She took her seat in the front row, surrounded by classmates. The bleachers had been split, one side roaring for Shadley, the other clad in the green of Xavier's.

Then came the Xavier's team.

The opposing team marched onto the court, each of them in deep green jerseys, tall and cut like they were born under weight racks and war chants. Among them, one stood out, the captain.

Siddharth Bhatia.

He looked like he belonged in a cologne ad, chiseled jawline, boulder shoulders, hair that didn't dare fall out of place, and a voice that could crack a stadium mic.

"Hi. Siddharth Bhatia. Captain, Xavier's," he said, holding out his hand. It was heavier than I expected, both the voice and the handshake.

"Hriday Raghuwanshi. Captain, Shadley," I replied, jaw set, eyes locked.

Was I jealous? Hell, yeah. He looked older. Broader. Like testosterone on legs. But I wasn't about to back down, I had heart. Fire. And I had *her* watching.

The referee, a seasoned man with a whistle you didn't argue with, stepped between us.

"Players, line up. Shake hands. Final huddle. Rules are simple, two ten-minute quarters. No fouls near the rim. No backcourt violations. Fast breaks allowed. Three-dribble serve, clean toss. Respect the whistle. Bad sportsmanship gets benched."

He paused, then added: "Ten minutes to tip-off. Gear up. And give us a game to remember."

We broke. I jogged to the coach, chest heaving, but eyes scanning the stands.

There she was, Arohi, cheeks flushed with excitement, eyes never leaving me. Her smile felt like victory in advance.

And yeah, I might've flexed just a little harder when I turned away. I knew I looked good, white jersey fitted tight, number 9 on my back, sweat catching the light. Siddharth could have the biceps, I had the moment.

The referee blew the whistle, a sharp sound that cut across the court like a blade.

Game on.

The court fell into a hush, then a rising wave of cheers as we gathered at the centre. Mohak clapped my back.

"Let's do this, Hriday!"

The referee nodded.

"Captains. Ball in."

He tossed the ball high. Time snapped.

I leaped, lungs wide, arms stretched like wings, and tipped the ball clean to Mohak, who caught it mid-run. He dribbled, dashed, passed to Aryan near the arc.

"Cut left!" I shouted.

Aryan faked, spun, sent it back. I caught, pivoted, launched, a perfect three-pointer. The ball arced high, kissed the rim, then fell clean through.

3–0. Shadley.

The crowd *exploded.*

Arohi leapt to her feet, clapping, her voice lost in the roar. My heart raced, not from the shot, but from the way she looked at me just then.

Siddharth's team rebounded, tried a fast break, but Mohak blocked the drive like a *beast,* sent it flying to me. I caught it, dashed down court, faked two defenders, and *slam dunked.*

5–0. Shadley again.

The court thundered.

But Xavier's weren't here to lose.

They regrouped like pros. In the final three minutes of the first quarter, they came back hard. Fast passes, aggressive screens, full-court press. Siddharth landed a deep three, their point guard cut inside for a slick layup, and then they stole possession off a bad pass and finished it with a clean jump shot.

5–3. Then 5–5. Then 5–8.

Xavier's had claimed the quarter.

The whistle blew, shrill, cold, commanding.

I looked to the stands. Arohi's hands were clenched together, her brows furrowed, but her eyes, her eyes still held fire for me.

This wasn't over. This was war. And I was just getting started.

SIDDHARTH

It was game day, and I had come to face the Shadley, our biggest rivals.

Everyone always said I had a knack for reading the game before it happened. Teammates called it instinct. Coach said it was vision. Truth is, I never really knew what to call it. It was just something inside me, this strange pulse that told me how things were going to unfold before the first whistle even blew.

But today... something felt different.

As I tightened the laces on my shoes and glanced towards the bleachers, I saw her.

She was sitting alone, first row from the court. Even from that distance, something about her hit me, hard. She wasn't cheering, or scrolling through her phone like everyone else. She was just sitting there, still... watching me.

Our eyes met.

And in that instant, everything else faded.

I don't know how to explain it. I'd never seen her before, and yet I *knew* her. Not from some memory. From something else.

From the future.

I saw flashes. Images. Moments. Her walking through the rain barefoot. Her laughing in some café we hadn't been to yet. Her crying alone in the dark. Me, reaching for her hand like I'd done it a thousand times before.

And then the whistle blew. The second quarter began.

But I was already somewhere else, not lost in thought, but in something I couldn't control.

It wasn't just attraction. It wasn't even fate. It felt like a warning.

I could sense it the moment I stepped onto the court, the Shadleys were up to something.

Their starting lineup was unusually quiet during warmups, eyes locked, whispering in tight huddles. I've played enough games to know when a team is running something pre-planned, something targeted. But it didn't matter. I had the instincts. I always did.

As we circled up for the tip-off, the ball went high into the air, hanging in that split second of gravity like the calm before a storm. I jumped early, stretched my arm out past my defender, and tipped it just right. Clean win on the jump ball. We were off.

The game started fast, too fast. Full-court press from the Shadleys right away. I dribbled hard, scanned the floor, called for a high pick-and-roll, but they anticipated it. Hriday, their point guard, snatched the loose ball off a deflected pass and took off on a fast break. I chased, but he was gone, two steps ahead, smooth euro-step into a left-hand layup.

2–0.

Hriday grinned at me as he jogged back on defence. Cocky. But he earned it. I shook it off, exhaled, focused.

But then… I saw her again.

First row. Just behind the baseline. The girl from earlier.

Her hair swung as she moved to the beat of the music blasting from the speakers during a timeout. She laughed, clapped, even did a little dance with someone beside her. And just like that, my world, my game, paused.

She wasn't trying to be a distraction. But she was.

The prettiest distraction I'd ever seen.

I tried to refocus. Tried to call out plays, set screens, push the tempo. But my timing was off. My passes got sloppy. I missed a wide-open corner three, airballed a free throw, and got caught ball-watching while Hriday drained another pull-up jumper from the elbow.

Coach yelled. Teammates signalled. I nodded, pretended I was locked in. But I wasn't.

She cheered wildly when the Shadleys scored. Not aggressively, just with genuine joy. Like she didn't care who won. Like she was just happy to be alive in that moment.

And it messed me up completely.

By the final quarter, the gap was twenty-two.

Hriday ran the court like it was his show, sinking back-to-back threes, throwing flashy no-look passes, and walking off each time with that smug grin.

We lost.

As the buzzer echoed through the court and our coach ripped into us, all I could do was glance toward the stands.

She was still there. Still smiling.

And I knew, without a doubt, this wasn't the last time I'd see her. Because some losses don't end with the scoreboard.

Some… begin with them.

HRIDAY

We won.

We *finally* won the tournament of my dreams.

Beating the best basketball team in all of Delhi, that was something I had dreamed of for years. After sixteen long years, Shadley had done it. We were the champions.

As the final whistle blew, Mohak ran straight at me and hugged me so hard that we both fell to the ground, overwhelmed by joy. Moments later, Golu joined us, collapsing beside us on the court. The three of us lay there, laughing, crying, unable to believe what we had just achieved.

Then our coach walked up. He looked proud, more than I'd ever seen him before. He placed a hand on my shoulder and said, "It's a moment of pride. Shadley has finally won and under *your* captaincy." My heart was full.

And then, suddenly, my eyes caught something across the court.

Arohi.

She was dancing with Mahi, lost in the celebration. And in that moment, I realised something unexpected:

She looked even happier than I was.

Our eyes met across the noise and chaos, yet, in that moment, everything else faded.

She stepped towards me, her arms half open for a hug, but the roaring crowd pulled her back.

There was a strange, beautiful silence between us.

A silence filled with unsaid words and electric glances.

Mahi came by, gave me a quick congratulatory hug, but Arohi...

She just stood there, smiling at me. That same smile that undressed my soul.

Without a word, I reached for her hand and led her away, past the court, to the quiet, shadowed wall we used to sit by after practice.

She didn't say a thing the entire way. But her silence was loud, it said everything.

When we reached, I gently pinned her back against the wall, leaned in close, and whispered,

"Baby... why do you keep staring at me like that?"

She stepped in, just a breath away, her voice low and sinful, "Because you're enough to drive me insane... what more could I want when my boyfriend's the hottest man alive?"

Her gaze trailed over me slowly, like a flame tracing skin.

"The way you dribbled that ball..."

She bit her lip.

"...was pure seduction."

I cupped her face without thinking, drawn to her like a tide to the moon, and our lips locked.

Hard. Fierce. Breathless.

She melted into me, her fingers tangled in my wet hair, my jersey clinging to my skin as her hands slid beneath it.

I lifted her effortlessly by the thighs, holding her close as we kissed deeper, slower, like we were trying to memorise the taste of victory on each other's lips.

She scratched my back softly, pulling me closer still. And in that heated blur of sweat, breath, and heartbeats...

There was no crowd. No trophy. No noise.

Just her. Just me.

And the fire between our mouths.

AROHI

"I love it when you kiss me like that," I said softly, but before I could finish, Hriday was already leaning in again, pressing his lips to mine with that same sweet urgency that always made my heart race.

A few minutes later, he pulled back just enough to look at me and whispered, "I love doing the things you love."

I blushed, my cheeks warming under his gaze. He smiled and tucked a strand of hair behind my ear. "Arohi, let's celebrate today. It's a big day for me. I want you, me, Golu and Mohak, and please bring Mahi too."

I smiled but hesitated. "Sure, baby… but I was hoping we could have a little time alone. There's something I need to tell you."

Hriday looked at me gently. "Baby, it's always 'us'. Every single day. Tonight, I just want to share this happiness with the people who matter. I want to introduce you to Mohak and Golu, this time, as my girlfriend. They don't really know about us yet."

He kissed my forehead gently and held my hands. "We'll have our moment later, just you and me. If that's okay?"

I nodded, a little overwhelmed but touched. He always knew how to calm the storm inside me.

"Let's go?" he asked, holding out his hand.

I took it and smiled. I wanted to tell him what had been bothering me since our last meeting, but I didn't. Not today. This was his day, his moment. And I knew how much it meant to him.

We stepped out into the sun, and there they were, Mahi, Mohak and Golu, waiting for us. None of them really knew about us, but they would soon.

"Guys!" Hriday called out. "We're celebrating today, and you're all coming. No drama, Mahi, you too."

They laughed and agreed without question.

"We also have something interesting to share," Hriday added with a grin.

Mohak smirked. "I think we already know," he said, pointing to the faint lipstick mark on Hriday's neck.

Everyone burst out laughing. I hid my face, blushing, while Mahi teased me. "Well, it's pretty obvious what you two were up to."

"Okay, okay, let's meet by five. That good for everyone?" Hriday asked.

Everyone agreed. Just then, Madhav called Hriday over. Hriday squeezed my hand, leaned in, and kissed my forehead again.

"See you soon," he said softly.

I watched him walk away, still holding the warmth of his touch. I knew I had something to tell him, something that mattered. But not now. Today was about him, and I didn't want anything to take that away.

Mahi and I walked towards my car, our steps slow, the evening air buzzing with excitement behind us. I glanced back and saw the boys dancing, the trophy gleaming in their hands, their laughter echoing through the parking lot. And there he was, Hriday, caught in that moment of pure joy, his eyes glowing with pride. Watching him like that made my heart ache in the best way.

"Aru," Mahi said, nudging me lightly, "when are you finally going to tell me what's going on between you and Hriday?"

I smiled to myself. "It all happened so fast, Mahi. But you'll know everything tonight, I promise."

She gave me a playful look, raising an eyebrow. "Okay, I'll hold you to that."

I looped my arm through hers. "Mahi, stay over tonight? It's been forever since we had a proper sleepover."

Her face lit up. "Sounds perfect."

"I'll just text Aunty that you're crashing at my place," I said, pulling out my phone. She nodded. "Done. She'll be cool with it."

Not long after, we were home, just the two of us, with a night ahead full of laughter, secrets, and everything waiting to be said.

"It's already 4.30, Mahi!" I shouted from the living room, glancing at my phone. "Hriday just messaged, they've already left their place."

"Coming, coming!" she called back. "Just a swipe of lipstick and I'm done!"

I rolled my eyes. "Hurry up, Mahi. For the last time, Mohak's not interested in you." She strutted out, unfazed. "Neither am I, sweetheart," she shot back with a wink.

Minutes later, we were rushing to the car. I slid into the backseat and asked our driver to take us to the metro station.

Mahi frowned. "The metro? Why the subway, Arohi? We could just drive straight there."

I gave her a soft, almost pleading smile. "I don't want to take the car today. Please, honey, trust me on this."

She sighed dramatically, but her smile said she'd follow me anywhere. "Alright, as you say, Bestie."

As the metro hummed beneath us, I typed out a quick text to Hriday: "We've boarded the metro too, baby. Will be there any moment now."

Within seconds, his reply popped up, a single kiss emoji.

Simple.

But it made my heart flutter.

HRIDAY

I walked into Café Delhi Heights with my boys, Golu and Mohak, right behind me. The place had that easy vibe and served almost every cuisine under the sun, which was perfect for the chaos our appetites usually brought with us.

Just as we grabbed a corner table, my phone buzzed. Arohi had texted, they were on the metro. I stared at the screen for a moment, a half-smile tugging at my lips.

"You know what's wild?" I said, turning to Golu and Mohak. "Arohi's got a whole fleet of cars parked outside that palace she calls a home, and still, she chooses to ride the metro. Just like she takes the bus to school every day, even though her family could've sent her in a chauffeur-driven BMW."

Mohak looked up from the menu, clearly impressed. "Wow," he said with genuine awe. "That girl's something else."

And yeah, she really was.

Golu had been suspiciously quiet the whole time, not because he didn't care about my love life (okay, maybe he didn't), but because his entire soul was buried in the menu. While Mohak and I talked, he was mentally tasting every dish on the list.

"Hriday," he finally groaned, "can we order already? These girls take *forever*."

Mohak laughed. "Madhav, relax. They'll be here any moment now. Meanwhile, make a list of everything you want, we'll order once they arrive."

Golu nodded like a disciplined toddler who'd been handed crayons and a colouring book. Mohak and I shared a look, both trying not to laugh.

And then… I felt her.

Even before I saw her, I *felt* her. Like some part of my heart already knew, *she's here*. I turned around, and there she was, walking through the entrance of the café like the whole place existed just to frame her.

The giant ceiling fan near the doorway caught her hair just right, sending it flying back like she was the heroine of a slow-motion Bollywood scene. She had slipped into a short yellow dress this time, bright as sunshine, and somehow made it look effortless. I stared. Of course I did. I always lost myself the moment I saw her.

She waved, and I motioned her to come join us.

Mohak immediately nudged Golu. "Move, man. Let her sit here," he whispered, eyeing the seat next to me.

"But why *me*?" Golu asked, completely baffled. "I got here first!"

"It's okay," I started, trying to de-escalate the situation.

But Mohak gave Golu *that look*, you know, the "don't mess with me" one. Golu sighed like a martyr and shuffled over with exaggerated drama.

The girls reached, both beaming. Arohi slid into the seat next to me, and everything else in the café just faded out. We all placed our orders, except for Golu, of course, who ordered enough to feed a small army.

"Bro, are you planning to invite the kitchen staff to join us too?" Mohak teased. Golu shrugged, unapologetic. "Just covering my emotional hunger."

We all laughed.

But me? I couldn't stop looking at the girl in the yellow dress who somehow made a crowded café feel like our own private world.

Mahi was the first to break the comfortable silence, nudging me with her elbow and flashing a mischievous grin.

"Alright, spill the tea already!" she said dramatically.

Golu looked utterly confused. "Which tea? We haven't even ordered chai yet…" Everyone burst into laughter.

"Duffer!" Mahi rolled her eyes. "By 'tea', I mean *how* these two ended up together. What happened? When? We need *details*, please!" she added with a wink.

Arohi gasped, "Shhh, Mahi! There's nothing to tell!" Her voice was soft but her cheeks were already giving her away.

Mohak leaned back with a sly smile. "Yeah… I don't think so." He winked in my direction.

Everyone turned to me now.

So I leaned in, rested my arms on the table, and began. "Okay, fine. But only because you all are too annoying to ignore."

I looked at Arohi, who was already halfway hiding behind her hair, and smiled before continuing.

"You know, when you truly fall for someone… it's never one moment. It's a hundred little ones that pile up, day after day, until one day, you're just… hers. Completely."

The table grew quiet.

"I don't remember the exact day I fell for her. Maybe it was when she raised her hand in class and shut the teacher up with that one-line sass. Or maybe it was when she tied her hair in that stupid half-bun and still looked like a goddess. Maybe it was the way she never tried to stand out, but somehow always did. She's chaos and calm. Loud when she wants, quiet when it matters. She made me *feel*, and I hadn't felt in a long time."

For a moment, I forgot we weren't alone.

Even Golu, with a huge burger in both hands, had watery eyes now. "Bro, I didn't sign up to cry and chew," he mumbled, and we all laughed.

"And the best part?" I added, looking at Arohi now. "I don't just see her in my present. I see her in every version of my future. Every city, every house, every dream. It's always her."

Arohi didn't say a word. But that didn't bother me. She didn't *have* to say it.

I knew she loved me, *more* than I could ever explain. Her silence spoke louder than any confession.

Mahi pulled her into a hug, wiping away a tear that had betrayed her cool-girl image. "Hriday," she said softly, "You're perfect for my best friend. I always knew it."

I raised an eyebrow, "*Always* knew?"

Arohi's eyes widened in panic as she glared daggers at Mahi. "Mahi… shut up!" she whispered sharply, cheeks now tomato-red.

But I wasn't letting it slide. "Nope. You're finishing that sentence. Out loud."

Mahi grinned like a kid about to spill a forbidden secret. "Fine. Arohi has been in love with you since *day one* at Shadley. She used to secretly stare at you during assemblies. Everyone at the table exploded in surprise.

I turned to Arohi, who had now buried her face in her hands, completely flushed. "*Really?*" I whispered, half laughing, half melting. "You little stalker."

Golu and Mohak jumped in, dramatically placing hands over their hearts. "And here we thought *you* were the obsessed one, Hriday!"

"Turns out it was mutual stalking all along!"

We all laughed again, but somewhere in between the jokes, I caught Arohi looking at me.

Eyes soft. Still. Unmoving.

And I knew, right there, right then, that this wasn't just a teenage story. It was something deeper. Something lasting.

And as chaos continued around the table, my world narrowed down to just her. And this time, *she didn't look away.*

4 March 2021

MADHAV

It was just another ordinary Monday. The kind when the classroom felt too familiar, the teachers too monotonous, and the windows too tempting. I was half-listening to the chemistry lecture, doodling aimlessly on my notebook, when the classroom door creaked open.

Heads turned. Even the teacher paused mid-sentence. There he stood.

Tall. Sharp. Silent.

His presence hit like a drop in pressure, like the room had exhaled all at once but forgotten how to breathe again. He wasn't trying to make an entrance, and yet somehow, he *did*. Eyes too calm, too unreadable. A navy-blue backpack slung over one shoulder. Rolled-up sleeves. That subtle, calculated confidence you don't learn, you're born with.

"Siddharth Bhatia," the teacher announced, flipping through the register. "Transferred from St. Xavier's. He'll be joining you for the rest of the year."

Xavier's. The name was enough to stir whispers. The school was elite, infamous for two things: excellent academics… and scandalous discipline records.

He walked in, gaze scanning the room like he was sizing everyone up. His eyes paused, just for a heartbeat, on Hriday.

Something unreadable passed between them.

A flicker. A crackle.

History? Rivalry? Or just a silent dare?

Siddharth took the empty seat at the back, tossing his bag onto the desk as if it didn't weigh a thing. He didn't say a word, didn't introduce himself. But even in silence, he screamed disruption.

I glanced at Hriday. His jaw had tightened. He wasn't smiling anymore. Even Mohak looked unusually quiet.

And then, Siddharth's eyes met mine.

It wasn't soft. It was... curious. A gaze that asked a question without forming it. A gaze that studied you like a puzzle.

And just like that, I felt something shift.

Like this year... was no longer going to go as planned.

SIDDHARTH

I never planned to come to Shadley.

Honestly, the very idea used to bore me. Polished walls, perfect uniforms, and students too comfortable in their own routine lives. I belonged to Xavier's. Where the chaos was raw, and no one played nice.

But then, *I saw her.*

It was the inter-school basketball tournament.

Yellow Lakers' jersey, tucked just enough to make your heart trip. Denim skirts that looked like sin. And those golden studs that moved when she did.

Arohi.

She wasn't cheering like the others. She was just... *watching*. Calm. Composed. Untouched by the noise around her.

And then she smiled.

Not at me. Not even in my direction. But *God*... that smile.

I swear something rewired in my brain in that exact moment.

That night, I didn't sleep. The next day, I couldn't focus. My friends called me insane when I told them I needed to find out who she was.

But I did.

Arohi Khanna. Shadley. Class 12-B. And the more I found out, the worse it got. That laugh. That confidence. The stories. The way people said her name like she was some campus legend.

I couldn't take it.

So, I made a decision.

Pulled some strings. Changed school mid-year. Transferred. Just like that.

Everyone thought I was running from trouble. Maybe I was. But not the kind they imagined. I wasn't running, I was *chasing*.

That match changed everything for me. She didn't even notice me, but I noticed *everything* about her. And I knew I couldn't go back to my old life. I had to be where she was.

I laugh, but it's hollow. Cold.

She's different. She doesn't even realise it, and maybe that's what kills me. The way she doesn't know the kind of effect she has. But I'm not here to admire her from across the room.

I step forward.

I'm here to make her *mine*.

HRIDAY

It was one of those lazy winter afternoons at school, the kind where the sun hit just right, warming the corridors, and everything felt slower, softer, and slightly unreal.

The last bell had rung, and the classrooms were emptying out, but I stayed back, pretending to search for something in my locker. Truth be told, I was waiting. For *her*.

And like magic, there she was. Arohi.

Walking down the hallway alone, her steps light but sure, hair tied in a messy ponytail that somehow made her look like trouble and poetry all at once. She wore that navy blue sweater that clung just right, the pleated skirt dancing around her knees. She hadn't seen me yet.

I stepped out, casually leaning against the locker. "Waiting for someone?" I asked, voice low.

She paused, a slow smile curving her lips. "Depends… is someone waiting for me?"

I grinned. "Always."

She looked away, biting her lower lip like she was trying not to smile, and damn, it made me want to close the distance between us even more.

"You know you're not allowed to make that face in school corridors," I whispered, walking towards her slowly.

"What face?"

"The one that makes me want to break every school rule."

Her breath hitched just a little, enough for me to notice. We stood now, just inches apart, the echo of voices fading away in the distance. Her back brushed against the wall of lockers as I leaned in, not touching her, but close enough for her to feel the heat between us.

"Hriday..." she whispered, almost like a warning, almost like an invitation. "Hmm?" I tilted my head, eyes on hers.

She was blushing now, cheeks a shade too pink. "We're in school."

"Exactly," I said. "We've got walls, a corner, and time. That's all I need."

She laughed, trying to look away, but I gently tilted her chin up, my thumb grazing the side of her face. Her skin was soft, warm. For a moment, we just looked at each other. No games, no teasing, just that kind of silence where everything is loud inside you.

And then, I bent down, brushing my lips gently over hers once, soft, teasing.

She gasped, and I smiled against her mouth. "You taste like mischief," I murmured.

"You taste like trouble," she shot back.

We kissed again, deeper this time, her fingers curling into my collar as if she needed something to hold on to. The world outside the corridor could burn for all I cared.

In that moment, it was just me, her, and the secret that tasted sweeter than any teenage dream.

We decided to stay back after classes, just the two of us, wanting to steal a little more time before the world pulled us back into routine. I remembered Arohi had wanted to share something with me the other day, so I turned to her, softly asking, "What was it you were about to tell me then?"

She grew quiet for a moment, her fingers nervously playing with the edge of her notebook. Then, with a deep breath, she finally spoke.

"That evening… when you dropped me home… I know I acted strange, Hriday. But please trust me, I'm not really like that."

Her voice wavered, and I could feel something heavier lying beneath her words.

"It's just that going back to that house feels like walking into a showroom, not a home. Everything's polished, expensive, cold. Conversations are about business deals and brand names, not feelings or memories. I'm tired of being introduced as 'the Khannas'. I'm not some trophy for display." She looked away, blinking quickly. "I don't want a life built on money. I want love… moments that make my heart feel full. I want to live, Hriday, not like a girl with a perfect last name, but as someone who finds joy in the little things. The smell of old books, the chaos of street food stalls, the comfort of sitting beside someone who really sees me. I don't enjoy the privileges they think I should. I crave simplicity. I crave real."

Her voice broke as the tears finally spilled. Watching her, fragile and brave all at once, made something inside me ache.

I gently cupped her face, wiping the tears from her cheeks with my thumbs. "Arohi, you don't ever have to explain yourself to me. I see you, not the last name, not the house, not the lifestyle. Just you. And believe me, that version of you, the one who smiles at sunsets, who laughs like a child when she sees puppies, who talks to plants, is the most beautiful thing I've ever known."

She let out a shaky laugh, and I leaned in, our foreheads touching.

"I don't want a perfect life either," I whispered. "I want one where we're together. I want to make you smile when you're sad, bring you chai when it rains, take you to the sea when you feel suffocated. Whatever makes you happy, Arohi, I'll do it. And when you forget how to smile, I'll be right there, reminding you with all the love I have."

She wrapped her arms around me tightly, like she never wanted to let go. And in that moment, I held her even closer, kissed her forehead gently, and promised her silently, this is your home now, right here, with me.

SIDDHARTH

I never wake up this early for these stupid classes, I thought, dragging myself out of bed in my marble-floored, temperature-controlled, unnecessarily oversized room. My watch blinked at me like it was judging my life choices. 7.02 a.m. Gross.

I stretched, walked past the full-length mirror (yes, I looked like a million bucks even with bed hair), and smirked. "Today's the day," I muttered, splashing cold water on my face. "Siddharth Bhatia is finally gonna do something *not* on his schedule, like confess his damn feelings."

I threw on my favourite cologne, *subtle expensive*, not *I'm-trying-too-hard expensive*, and grabbed my keys. The Bentley could rest today. I was taking the campus Jeep. Needed to keep it *casual.*

I laughed under my breath. Arohi's probably going to roll her eyes when I tell her. I adjusted my cuffs, grabbed my black coffee (no sugar, no drama), and looked out at the driveway.

"She's different," I said to no one. "She doesn't give a damn that my last name unlocks boardrooms. She looks at me like I'm just *me.* And I swear, when she smiles, everything else just… blurs."

I stepped into the morning sun, flashing a grin to the sleepy guard at the gate. "Wish me luck, Bhaiya. Gonna tell a girl she's got the whole damn Bhatia heir wrapped around her little finger."

This wasn't just another conquest. This wasn't about charm or games. This was Arohi. And I was all in.

As I walked into school, something shifted. There she was. Arohi.

Laughing with her friends near the corridor. God, that laugh, it wasn't even loud, but it hit different. Like sugar melting into coffee. She looked so alive in that moment, like nothing around her could dull her sparkle.

And just like that, the usual swagger I carried everywhere? Gone. My shoulders tensed. My heart? Racing like I was about to walk into a boxing ring. Which was ridiculous, because I'm *Siddharth Bhatia*. Confident. Completely unshakable. People don't make *me* nervous.

Except her.

Still, I walked over. Eyes locked on her, so obviously that one of her friends noticed and whispered, "New boy's here."

I didn't even glance at them. I wasn't here for commentary. I was here for *her*.

"Hey, Arohi," I said, voice calm on the surface but my chest? Chaos. "Can I take a moment of yours?"

She looked at me, eyes soft but guarded. "May I know the reason?"

I froze. Words just… slipped out of my brain. I, who had navigated dates, rejections, and attention like a pro, was suddenly blank. Silent.

But she noticed. She *felt* it. She read something in my silence and nodded gently. "Okay," she said. "Let's walk."

And we did. Just a few quiet steps away from the noise, but enough to feel like the air changed.

Being close to her… man. That subtle scent, Gucci Flora. It hit me like a memory I never had. I don't usually get shy, you know? I've had fourteen exes. Fourteen. But none of them ever made my hands cold or my thoughts race like this.

Come on, Siddy, I told myself. *You're a Bhatia. And Bhatias don't fear. They conquer.*

I took a breath. Looked at her.

"Arohi," I said, finally. "I genuinely like you."

She looked at me for a beat. Then, with all the kindness in the world, said, "Siddharth, right? Do I even know you? Nonetheless, I love someone else. Hriday. I care about him, truly. And I wouldn't want to hurt you by pretending otherwise. Please… don't come between us."

It didn't sting the way rejections usually do. Maybe because she said it so sincerely. Maybe because I already knew what her answer would be. But still... hearing it hit different.

I smiled. Just a little. Just enough.

"Got it," I said. "No hard feelings, Arohi. But between us? I don't give up easy."

"Come on, let's at least be friends," I said, trying to keep it light, though my heart wasn't all that casual about it. She looked at me for a second, then smiled, one of those small, hesitant ones. "Okay," she said, and we shook hands. In that brief moment, something shifted, maybe not everything I wanted, but enough to keep me standing there with a smile of my own.

I didn't feel defeated. I felt... *certain*. Because some stories take time. And I knew, deep down, ours had only just begun.

Two Months Later

MADHAV

It was one of those days when the classroom felt heavier than usual, not because of the heat, but the silence. Most of our classmates were out during the free period, pretending to be in the library or on bathroom breaks that lasted forever. But I stayed back, partly because I wanted a break from the noise, but mostly because Hriday was doing the same.

He sat two benches ahead, elbows resting on the desk, spinning his pen like he always did when his mind was elsewhere.

"Hey," I called out, shifting from the window seat to one closer to him. He turned, eyebrows raised, and greeted me with that casual smirk. "What's up, Golu?"

I sat down beside him, letting the silence hang for a beat before I said it. "I don't know, man… I've been meaning to ask you something."

He looked at me, a bit more alert now.

"What is it?" he asked, brows furrowed slightly.

"I mean…" I hesitated, scratching the back of my neck, "…everything okay between you and Arohi?"

He blinked, almost confused for a moment. Then he smiled, *that* smile. The one he gets when she's on his mind.

"Everything's perfect," he said, nodding. "Actually… more than perfect. These past two months with her? They've been the best days of my life."

I leaned back, watching his face light up as he spoke. He didn't need to say it; I could see it written all over him.

"Last week," he started, grinning, "she made me sit through that lame rom-com she loves, you know, the one with that guy who keeps missing the train and ends up finding love in the most ridiculous way? I thought I'd die of boredom."

He laughed, shaking his head.

"But then she tucked her hand under my arm halfway through the movie, and I don't know, man… suddenly even that nonsense plot felt like magic."

I smiled faintly.

"Yesterday, she made me wait outside the class with a note stuck to my book, 'You forgot your dose of me today, idiot', and when I turned around, she was standing behind me with those cupcakes from L'Opéra Bakery. Who even does that? Arohi does."

He looked down at his fingers, the smile softening. "We've been through our share of weird fights too, like when I forgot our one-month anniversary and she didn't talk to me for two days. But even that ended with a kiss outside the basketball court. In the rain."

His words were soaked in warmth, the kind of warmth only love could give. But even with all that… something in me tugged uncomfortably.

I let out a low breath.

"I'm happy for you, Hriday. You know that, right?"

"Yeah, I know."

"But..." I paused. "Don't get me wrong… it's just… I feel something's off."

His smile faded slightly, his eyes narrowing just a little. "Off? Like what?"

I looked around the empty classroom, then leaned in.

"I've been noticing… Arohi and Siddharth, they've been talking more lately. Sitting together during breaks, laughing over things, staying back even after classes sometimes. I don't know, bro… It could be nothing. But it doesn't feel like nothing."

Hriday tilted his head, expression unreadable for a moment. Then he leaned back and sighed.

"She told me about him, Golu," he said calmly. "That they're just friends. And honestly, I believe her. Siddharth's a good guy, smart, chill. He knows we're dating. He wouldn't cross a line."

I watched him, the way he said it so firmly. But there was a flicker, *the tiniest one*, in his voice, like he was trying to convince himself too.

I didn't want to poke him any further.

"If you're fine, then I'm fine," I said finally. "If you're happy, then I'm happy too. Just… keep your eyes open, alright?"

He smiled, but this time it didn't quite reach his eyes.

The classroom door creaked as a breeze pushed it wider, the sound sharp in the silence. Hriday turned to look at it and muttered, almost to himself, "I always do."

The bell rang, echoing through the corridor, and soon our classmates started filing into the room. I watched as Arohi walked in, her steps light, and without a word, she wrapped her arms around Hriday from behind. He smiled instantly, like her touch flipped some hidden switch in him, and the two of them settled into their usual spot, comfortable, like nothing else existed.

But my eyes, my damn eyes, got stuck on Siddharth. The way he was watching them… not casually, not blankly. It was too focused, too lingering.

Just then, Mohak dropped into the seat beside me. I leaned towards him, still glaring at Siddharth.

"I swear, Mohak," I muttered, "I feel like punching Sid right in the face for staring at them like that."

Mohak, ever the peacemaker, shrugged. "Sid's a nice guy, man. He won't cross the line."

I rolled my eyes so hard it hurt. *Great.* Another one reciting the same line like it's written on his forehead. Hearing it again, from *this* idiot too, only added fuel to the fire burning inside me.

I made a face at him and turned away, choosing silence over arguing with someone who clearly wasn't seeing what I saw.

Just then, I saw Dijvijay Sir walk into our classroom, clutching a sheet of paper behind his back, the way he always did when he had something important to say.

"Students," he began, clearing his throat, "let me read out a very important notice to you."

Before he could even finish the sentence, the classroom buzzed with low murmurs and guesses.

"Silence!" he shouted, his voice cutting through the noise like chalk against a board. "Or I'll cancel the plan before even announcing it."

That shut us up.

He straightened the piece of paper and continued, "The school has planned a ten-day educational trip to Mussoorie, leaving on the 28th of next month. There will be nature walks, a short trek to George Everest, a local culture exploration, and yes... a night camp under the stars."

Gasps, cheers, and excited whispers erupted.

"Interested students," he added, scanning the room, "can give their names to Madhav. He will be coordinating the list."

My heart did a backflip. A wide smile stretched across my face, I couldn't help it. *Of all people, he picked me.* Not Hriday, not Mohak. Me. The room suddenly felt brighter.

Everyone was instantly on fire with plans.

Within minutes, groups had formed, voices rising with excitement. Bags were already being packed, in their heads, at least. Plans for tents, cabins, seat partners on the train, playlists, snacks, and late-night games were flying across desks.

In one corner, Arohi and Mahi had huddled up, pulling out their phones and discussing outfits like they were prepping for a fashion week instead of a school trip.

"I swear, I'm only wearing pastels," Mahi said dramatically.

"And I'm packing my oversized hoodie," Arohi added, "only because Hriday steals it every time."

They both giggled, completely lost in their own little world of daydreams and fabrics.

Hriday, sitting nearby, pretended not to listen, but the smile playing at the corners of his lips gave him away.

"You know I'm not giving it back this time," he murmured, making Arohi throw a pen cap at him.

"Try me," she smirked.

Meanwhile, Siddharth, from across the room, looked up at all of this, the laughter, the pairing off, the glowing faces, and there was something unreadable in his eyes.

Something quiet. Something brewing.

And just like that, the trip to Mussoorie was no longer just a school outing. It was the beginning of something none of us saw coming.

HRIDAY

I was standing just outside the basketball court when I saw Arohi stepping out, her hair tied up, cheeks a little flushed from the game. My heart skipped a beat.

"Babe, you're here?" I said, grinning with excitement.

She smiled, already reading the look in my eyes. "Just wanted to surprise you."

"Mohak helped me," she added, winking. "I asked him when you'd be here."

Without wasting another second, I pulled her in by the waist, her laughter spilling into the air as our bodies met. I brushed a soft kiss on her cheek, and just when my hands began to slide under the hem of her top, she held my wrist and whispered, "Babe… come inside. Make me play basketball today."

"Anything for you," I said, already falling all over again.

We walked onto the court, just the two of us under the open sky and the echo of bouncing balls from far away. I passed her the ball, and she tried to dribble, missing her step on purpose, giggling the entire time.

"Terrible form," I teased.

"Then help me, Coach," she replied, mock serious.

She aimed for the basket but couldn't quite reach. "Lift me!" she said, eyes twinkling.

I didn't even hesitate. My hands slid around her waist as I lifted her into the air like she weighed nothing. Her fingers guided the ball through the hoop. She let out the cutest cheer as I slowly lowered her, not letting her feet touch the ground right away.

We ended up near the half-court line, breathless from laughter. She leaned into me, both of us slightly sweaty and glowing under the golden court lights. I cupped her face and kissed her – slow, sweet, the kind that makes time pause. Her fingers tangled into my hair as she deepened it, playful and full of warmth.

"You're so bad at basketball," I whispered against her lips.

"And you're so good at distracting me," she replied, biting back a smile.

We stood there in our own world, sneakers scuffing the court, hearts beating louder than the bouncing of any ball. And in that moment, the only game that mattered was the one where we kept falling for each other, again and again.

SIDDHARTH

I don't even know when it happened, when a simple friendship with Arohi turned into this... obsession. This constant ache in my chest.

She's everywhere now. In my thoughts, in my dreams, in the way I smile at my phone every time her picture pops up. The past few months have been nothing short of magic. We've hung out more than ever, laughed until our stomachs hurt, shared moments that felt like something more, at least to me. And when I see her beside me in photos, it *feels* right. Like we belong. Like the universe is trying to tell me something.

But then there's Hriday. The one she loves. And it kills me.

Still… I can't back down. I won't.

I love her, madly, deeply, helplessly. And I know, somewhere deep in her heart, she feels something too. She has to.

I don't care who she says she loves. What matters is who *loves her the most*. And that's me.

I'm done waiting.

When we're in Mussoorie, I'm going to tell her. Ask her out, one last time. No more holding back. No more pretending to be okay with just being the friend.

This time, I'm going all in.

Because if she's meant to be mine…

I'll fight the world for her. Even if it means losing myself.

28 May – Mussoorie Express

HRIDAY

"Hriday, I've packed some snacks for all of you. Don't finish them in one go, they need to last ten days," Maa said while stuffing the last zip of my over-packed bag.

"Yes, Maa! Don't worry. We'll ration like it's a war zone," I laughed, hurriedly shoving clothes into my suitcase in the most chaotic way possible.

"And tell Arohi I packed some theplas for her. She loves them."

I paused and smiled. Maa *knew*. She didn't need to say anything more. The look on her face already held a thousand soft approvals. Mothers always know.

"Dad will drop you and Golu," she added.

"Mohak too, Maa," I reminded her.

"Ohh that's nice! Please take care of yourself, Beta. And *send pictures!* I'll miss you," she said, her voice cracking a bit.

I gave her the tightest hug, the kind that makes you forget for a second that you're eighteen and way too cool to cry.

Fast forward an hour, and we were at Hazrat Nizamuddin Station, chaotic as ever, students swarming around like ants on sugar, and our PT teacher blowing his whistle like he was controlling traffic at Times Square.

Just as I looked around, something shifted, like my heartbeat got Wi-Fi signal.

And then I saw her.

Arohi. Dressed in the cutest baby-blue co-ord set, hair bouncing as she pulled a suitcase almost bigger than her, *Samsonite* proudly gleaming like it had a personality.

I was still mid-admiration when Golu elbowed me hard.

"Oye lover boy, stop drooling. Siddharth's out here doing a catwalk with his Gucci duffel and Ray-Ban shades. Flexing like it's a fashion week."

I couldn't care less. Because Arohi walked straight to me, looked me dead in the eye, and said, "I'm sleeping with you tonight, Babe."

I swear, my soul left my body. I probably blushed hard enough to light up the platform.

I blew her a flying kiss, which Golu tried to catch mid-air and dramatically *threw back* at me.

Just then, the announcement blared: "Train number 14041 Mussoorie Express to Dehradun will arrive on platform number 6 at 7 p.m."

And to everyone's shock, *drumroll please*, it was actually on time. Somewhere, Indian Railways was flexing harder than Siddharth's Louis Vuitton belt.

We all clambered into our bogies, me, Arohi, Golu, Mohak, Mahi, and yes, even the ever-so-fabulous Siddharth, and squeezed into our section of seats like a stack of emotional Pringles.

The vibe? Immaculate. Laughter, card games, selfies, roasted peanuts, chaos. We were a walking teenage movie.

After a while, Arohi leaned her head on my chest, eyes fluttering shut.

I blew her a soft kiss, gently brushing a few strands of hair from her face. She looked tired, like the kind of tired that deserved to be pampered. So I held her close, whispering sweet nonsense only she could hear.

Across from us, I caught Siddharth looking away. Didn't bother me. I was too busy being in love.

That's when Sid finally broke the silence. "Lucky you are, bro… getting a girl like Arohi."

Before I could respond, Mohak jumped in with his usual flair.

"And lucky *she* is, to get Hriday! Come on, man, have you seen this guy? Captain of the basketball team, can actually cook, doesn't ghost texts, AND smells like heaven."

"Yah bro! I mean, look at you and look at her…" Sid said, probably realising mid-sentence that he wasn't exactly helping himself.

That's when Golu stood up like a lawyer in court.

"And look at *you*! Having the guts to say this stuff out loud with that torn hoodie and oily hair. Bhai, read the room."

Everyone burst out laughing. Honestly, my friends? Absolute hype machines.

Just when the chaos peaked, Arohi stirred, groggy and confused. "Can you all *shut up*? Some of us are trying to sleep in peace!"

"Yes, Ma'am," we chorused like guilty schoolboys.

She looked up at me and mumbled, "Can I sleep in your lap?" Like I was going to say no.

I shifted, cradled her gently, and as the train began its slow rumble into the dark, we both drifted off, her heartbeat against my thigh, my hand softly holding hers. Somewhere in the background, Mahi snored, Golu was still munching chips, and Mohak quietly whispered, "True love, Bhai. True love."

After a ten-hour overnight ride, we finally rolled into Dehradun. One look at Arohi's sleepy-sunrise face and I felt myself falling for her all over again. She turned, eyes dancing despite the early hour, and whispered, "Babe, I know Mussoorie inside out, I'm going to show you everything." It wasn't her first trip, but it was our first trip together, and that made every detail feel brand new. I laced my fingers through hers, her suitcase in my other hand, and parked her with Mahi and the rest of the gang on the platform while I chased down my own luggage.

When I hurried back she'd vanished. Mohak waved me towards the exit, everyone had already boarded the bus for the last ninety-minute climb to Landour, where the school had booked an entire property. I clambered on and spotted Arohi curled by the window, half-asleep, Sid inching towards the seat beside her. Golu blocked him with a grin. "Hey, hey, move it. Hriday's back; that seat's his." I slid in, earning a drowsy smile as Arohi rested her head on my shoulder.

The road began to wind upwards, pine-scented air drifting through cracked windows. Arohi traced misty hearts on the glass and pointed out valleys just catching the first pink light; each time she leaned across me to share a view, her hair brushed my cheek like a promise.

We laughed when the bus lurched and she grabbed my arm for balance, neither of us letting go even after the wheels steadied.

Two quick pit stops for washrooms and steaming roadside parathas later, the bus finally turned into Woodlock Camping Villa, tucked beneath rhododendron canopies in Landour. As we stepped off, the mountains opened around us like an invitation, and I realised the real journey had only just begun, with her hand still warm in mine.

AROHI

"What an exhausting journey that was," I sighed to Hriday. With a teasing grin he answered, "So flights are better, right?" I laughed and declared, "I adore train rides too, especially when you're on them with me." He kissed the top of my head then, a tender reminder that to him, I was always the most important person in the room.

While Hriday went to collect our luggage, the staff handed out keys and room assignments. As expected, Mahi and I were placed together, our room nestled between Hriday and Mohak's on the left and Madhav and Sid's on the right. (Madhav tried to convince the teacher to switch partners, but the request was firmly denied.) The teachers informed us that the full itinerary was posted in each room and that punctuality for every activity was non-negotiable.

After Hriday saw me safely to my door and slipped back to his own, there was a knock on the door. Sid poked his head in. "Hey, girls, everything okay? If you need anything, I've got connections," he offered with a conspiratorial wink.

"No, thanks," Mahi replied, shutting the door.

"That was a little rude, Mahi, he was only being nice," I chided.

"Whatever," she muttered, collapsing onto the bed. "Read me the itinerary, will you?"

HRIDAY

A sudden loud bang on our door startled us, it sounded like someone was trying to break it down. When we opened it, there stood Golu, juggling his suitcase and a massive snack bag.

"I'm *not* sharing a room with that idiot," he announced with dramatic flair. "I'm moving in here. And before you ask, I come with snacks and zero apologies!"

We burst out laughing as Mohak rolled his eyes. "Come in, nuisance. You'd better have my favourite chips."

"Yes, Bhai!" Golu grinned, dropping his luggage with a thud. "Let's chill for a bit, then we've got that visit to the hilltop gardens and the old British church, right?"

We settled in. "Guys," he said, "I've been thinking... I want to plan a special date night for Arohi on the last day. Just the two of us, under the stars."

Mohak let out an excited yell. "Wohooo! That sounds crazy, Bhai!"

"Let me know if you need help, bro," Golu added, tossing him a wink.

I wanted to tell her everything that night. How being with her made the world feel right... how her laugh felt like a melody I wanted to keep hearing, and her presence, peaceful, chaotic, perfect, felt like home. I didn't think she even knew how much she meant to me. And in that moment, even Mohak didn't tease. We all just knew: love was about to write something unforgettable.

"Eyes Only for You"

HRIDAY

The sun had only just begun to lean westward when we all stirred from our afternoon naps. The villa, wrapped in a golden hush, came alive again with scattered footsteps and murmurs of laughter echoing down its marble corridors. A few of the gang were already gathering in the lounge, rubbing sleep from their eyes, settling back into familiar rhythms, half-asleep, half-charged.

But me?

I was somewhere else entirely.

Because the moment *she* walked in, time splintered. Arohi.

She didn't just *enter* a room; she *shifted* it. Dressed simply, white cotton shirt tucked lazily into denim shorts, damp hair curling at the edges from a quick shower, she looked like summer had taken human form. My eyes found her and refused to leave. Everyone else faded like background noise in a memory I didn't care to keep.

She caught my gaze, paused mid-step, and for a split second, it was just the two of us. Her lips parted, barely. My heartbeat thudded once, twice, too hard.

I crossed the room towards her without thinking, drawn by something feral, urgent. She tilted her head, a question lingering behind those eyes I could write sonnets about.

"You look like a dream I forgot I had," I whispered. My voice came out rougher than I meant.

She laughed softly, low and smoky. "Then you'd better wake up before you miss it."

I smiled, brushing a strand of hair behind her ear. "No. I think I'd rather get lost in it."

The rest of the evening spun around us, dinner, drinks, dancing on the patio, but for me, it was all a prelude. Every time our eyes met across the room, it was a spark thrown into dry leaves. Each accidental touch, each whispered joke, was a rope tightening between us. By night, I knew we wouldn't be able to stay apart.

The villa slept.

I slipped out of my room barefoot, every creaking floorboard a conspiracy. The night air was thick with jasmine and silence. I moved like a shadow down the hall, towards the back staircase. Our secret meeting place had been chosen earlier, with only a glance exchanged during dinner: the rooftop. The topmost part of the villa, barely known, barely touched. A place outside time.

And she was already there.

She stood under the stars, wind teasing her hair, the moonlight pouring down her like worship. When she turned, her eyes were already burning.

"You came," she whispered.

"I would've crossed galaxies."

Our mouths met like the collision of comets, slow at first, tasting, teasing. Her hands found my chest, fingers tracing patterns like poetry against skin. I pulled her closer, feeling every breath, every shiver as her body pressed against mine.

The world narrowed to lips and hands, to the rustle of clothing and gasped sighs. We sank to the blanket she'd laid out, smart, sensual Arohi, and I kissed every inch of her like I was memorising a map back to heaven.

Her laughter spilled like wine when I teased her neck with my teeth. "You're trouble," she whispered.

"I'm yours," I murmured against her collarbone. "So let me be trouble for you."

Skin against skin, the night wrapped around us like velvet. We moved slow, then fast, then slow again, like a dance only we knew. Her fingers clawed at my back when I kissed down her stomach; my breath caught when she whispered my name like a secret meant only for the stars.

It wasn't just about the pleasure, though, god, there was plenty of that, it was about the way she looked at me like I was the only man alive. About how she trembled, how she arched, how she *gave*. We weren't just making love; we were rewriting its definition.

And when it was over, our bodies tangled, our hearts still racing, we lay there beneath the vast, endless sky.

"Do you think," she said, her voice sleepy, "anyone will ever know what we did up here?"

"No," I said, pulling her closer. "And even if they did, they wouldn't *understand* it." She smiled and tucked herself into the curve of my body.

The stars blinked on above us like a blessing, and I knew this wasn't just a night.

It was the beginning of *everything*.

Nine days in Mussoorie felt less like a trip and more like a beautiful fever dream we never wanted to wake up from, sunrises at Lal Tibba, café hopping in Landour, drenching ourselves like wild kids at Kempty and Bhatta Falls, and losing track of time wandering through the misty trails of George Everest Peak. Every day carried its own chaos and charm, whether it was Golu and Mohak bickering over who clicked the better candid or Sid being an absolute pain in the ass, asking deep questions like "Do you think Wi-Fi travels faster in the hills?" while wearing socks with floaters. Mahi and Arohi brought the aesthetic to every photo while the boys brought noise, but somewhere between all the laughter and late-night Maggi, something softer bloomed, Arohi and I gravitated towards each other like gravity finally made sense. From sharing cinnamon rolls at Emily's Café to stolen glances during treks and quiet confessions during sunset strolls, it all led to that one unforgettable night when we snuck away to the hidden rooftop of our villa, far from the noise, under a sky painted with stars and secrets, where our kisses turned into something slow, breathless, and fiery. We didn't just fall for each other, we dove headfirst. The whole trip felt like a montage stitched with madness, mischief, and magic: dancing on the villa balcony with fairy lights and music no one else could hear, group selfies at Company Garden with half-closed eyes, Sid's unexpected crush on a spa therapist he claimed had "chakra-opening hands", and that one moment on Gun Hill when we all just stood in silence, knowing we'd never get days like these again. It wasn't just a vacation; it was a little lifetime.

It was the final day of our trip, a bittersweet morning laced with anticipation. The teachers had gifted us the whole day to ourselves, to wander wherever our hearts desired. But my heart had made its choice long before. I had planned a special day with Arohi, one that I hoped she'd never forget.

The night before, I had asked her softly, "Can I plan tomorrow for you?" She didn't hesitate, her eyes sparkled as she smiled and said yes.

I had arranged a secluded riverside spot, scattered with hundreds of tulips, her favourite. Every detail whispered her name.

At 9 a.m., I waited at the villa's exit, my heart skipping with every minute. By 9.20, I saw her. And time, it simply stopped.

She walked towards me in a flowing white dress, her hair half pinned back with a dainty bow, like something straight out of a fairytale. For a moment, I couldn't breathe. She looked like a dream that the morning sunlight had just conjured.

"I'm so sorry, Hriday, I'm late," she said, slightly breathless.

I smiled, still awestruck. "Pretty girls are never late, Arohi. They're just too busy being beautiful."

She giggled shyly and leaned in to kiss me gently on the cheek. "I always love you more in polo T-shirts, Hriday," she teased.

"Oh really? Then I guess I'll wear them till the day I die," I laughed. She laughed louder, the sound more musical than anything I'd ever heard.

I took her hands in mine. "Where are we going?" she asked with curiosity dancing in her eyes.

Placing a finger softly on her lips, I whispered, "Just be with me. You're going to love today."

We began at a hidden flower garden I'd found earlier in the trip. Her eyes lit up as she twirled among the blooms, arms open like she was flying. We lay in the soft grass under the morning sun, our fingers interlaced, our laughter echoing between the trees. I snapped photos, recorded her smile, captured every second, because I wanted to bottle this day forever.

We chased butterflies. She braided a tiny daisy into my hair. I picked a wildflower and tucked it behind her ear. We danced barefoot to no music at all. She sat on my lap and fed me strawberries from her little picnic bag. I whispered poems in her ear. She traced the lines of my palm and told me it felt like home.

At one point, she hovered above me, her hair cascading like silk, her face glowing. "Is this real?" she whispered.

"Only the most beautiful dreams are," I replied.

As the sun dipped beneath the horizon, painting the sky in hues of fire and gold, I gently kissed her forehead and said, "Be ready again by 9 tonight."

She looked at me, puzzled but glowing. "More? Hriday, today was everything."

Her eyes shimmered, glassy with emotion. "No one's ever made me feel like this before," she said softly. "Like I'm… the only girl in the world." A tear escaped down her cheek, and she smiled through it.

I wiped it tenderly. "Baby, you deserve the world, and more. Tonight, I want to see you in red... because reds are for special days right?"

She laughed through her tears. "You remember that?"

"Every little thing," I said, pulling her close.

I kissed her forehead. She stood on her toes, cupped my face, and kissed me, full and slow, on the lips.

And just like that, under a twilight sky, we parted for our rooms, hearts louder than ever, souls already tangled in the story we were writing together.

9 p.m.: The D-Day

I was ready, dressed in my black polo neck, the one Arohi always said she loved on me. I had told Golu everything, every detail of tonight. He even helped me come up with a few cliché lines to break the ice. We couldn't find Mohak; Mahi mentioned he'd stepped out for some snacks. No big deal, I thought.

I messaged Arohi: *"Babe, are you ready? Meet me at the gate."*

The message was delivered. I waited.

Ten minutes passed. Then twenty. At thirty, still no reply. The unease began to grow, slow but certain.

Just then, a friend walked by and asked if I'd seen Sid. Apparently, he needed some photos from him. I shook my head.

"He's been missing for over an hour," the friend muttered before walking off. "God knows where he is."

The words stuck. *Over an hour?* My heart started to beat differently now. A sudden, silent dread crept in. Was Sid… with Arohi?

But no, Arohi would have told me. She always did. Every time Sid crossed a line, she made sure I knew. That was our unspoken code. And yet tonight… silence. Nothing. Not a word.

Something didn't feel right.

I spotted Mahi hurrying down the corridor. "Have you seen Arohi?" I blurted out.

"I… I don't know what she's up to," she muttered, eyes darting away, before disappearing around the corner.

A cold current rippled through me. Something was wrong, terribly wrong, and for the first time a voice inside whispered that the night would refuse to bend to my plans.

I sent Golu to Arohi's room. He came back pale. "Locked."

"Try Sid's," I said, hating the thought even as it crossed my mind. He returned with the same answer: "Locked."

I rang her door-bell, once, twice, the chime echoing like taunts down the hallway. Twenty calls, fifty frantic messages, nothing. Arohi always told me where she went; the silence felt like a betrayal in itself. Two hours bled away while I paced our room, heartbeat hammering my ribs, sweat slick on my palms. Golu tried to soothe me, maybe she'd gone shopping somewhere without signal.

"Bhai, she would've told me," I snapped. "She never vanishes."

Before he could reply, a crashing sound thundered from Arohi and Mahi's room. Golu's eyes locked on mine: no one was supposed to be in there. Another thud followed, sharper, like furniture falling in haste.

"We're going in," I said. No hesitation, no second thoughts. From our balcony we could see theirs, the gap a single desperate leap over darkness. I clasped my hands to give Golu a boost, he vaulted across, landed, then reached back for me. I sprang after him, adrenaline drowning every rational fear.

We landed on Arohi's balcony. Inside, the curtains fluttered, shadows shifting. My pulse pounded loud enough.

I couldn't believe what I saw.

Golu was about to step inside, but I held him back with a trembling hand. My breath hitched, my heartbeat a deafening roar in my ears. There she was, Arohi, in that red dress I had gifted her on our two-month anniversary, the one she had called *her favourite*, the one she promised she'd wear only for me.

She wasn't alone.

The lights were dim, but I could see enough. His hands traced her waist. Her fingers clutched the back of his neck. Their lips moved feverishly, bodies tangled in a hunger I had once believed was ours. She let out a soft moan, one I knew too well. They weren't just kissing, they were lost in each other, shamelessly, breathlessly… like I never existed.

I stood frozen, unable to breathe, unable to think. My legs felt like they'd betray me any second. My chest caved in, piece by piece. The girl I had loved so deeply, blindly, was in someone else's arms, wearing the memory of me while creating one with him. She wasn't stopping him; she was holding him closer. The red fabric of her dress slipped slightly down her shoulder, and he leaned in, mouth trailing over her bare skin like it was something he had waited a lifetime to taste.

Tears rolled down without warning, burning as they fell. Golu wrapped his arm around me, steadying me as I almost collapsed.

"Hriday," he said softly, rage and sorrow simmering in his voice, "I told you… Sid was never a good guy. You loved her too much, Bhai. Way too much."

I felt myself take a step back, like my body couldn't bear to stay rooted in a moment that didn't belong to me. I couldn't speak. I was crumbling, helpless, watching the only person I had let into the deepest corners of my heart shatter it without mercy. Everything I had imagined for us… it all died in that single moment.

Then, like fate wasn't done tormenting me, we heard a voice from the room next to us.

"Hey Madhav! What are you guys doing in the girls' balcony?" We both turned, stunned.

It was Siddharth, standing in *his* room.

My blood ran cold. Golu's eyes widened in horror.

"Wait... if you're here," Golu stammered, "then who the hell is inside with Arohi?" The pieces no longer fit. The truth twisted in ways darker than betrayal.

Without another word, we both lunged at the balcony door and slammed it open with every ounce of strength we had.

The sound of the balcony door creaking open sliced through the heavy silence like a blade.

They froze.

Their lips, which just seconds ago had been locked in feverish hunger, parted. Their bodies, tangled like they couldn't bear a moment of distance, suddenly stiffened like statues caught under a spotlight. Arohi slowly turned her head towards the open door. The room was dark, barely any light, but she *knew*.

She could see me.

And I could see *everything*.

Her dress was crumpled around her waist, the straps slightly falling from her shoulders. Her breathing was erratic, chest rising and falling as she pushed herself away from him, straightening her posture, trying to make sense of the chaos, *our* chaos. Her fingers fumbled to fix the strap of the red dress I had once chosen so carefully for her. The one she had called "perfect for a forever memory".

She looked like she had seen a ghost, but not out of guilt. More like regret at being *caught*.

Then the other figure, the one she had just been kissing like he was her whole world, moved.

"Who the fuck is it now?" the voice grumbled in irritation.

That voice.

It hit me first in the gut. Familiar, casual, like hundreds of nights we'd spent playing music together, planning trips, sharing secrets.

The man stood up, bare-chested, turning towards me as he clicked the switch. The lights burst on.

I staggered.

"*No*..." I whispered.

My chest collapsed inwards.

"*Mohak?*" the name escaped my lips like it had betrayed me too. My best friend.

The same Mohak who hugged me the night I told him Arohi had agreed to be mine. The same Mohak who was supposed to be out getting snacks just an hour ago.

His eyes locked with mine. Wide, stunned… but not ashamed. "Hriday," Arohi's voice broke, trembling.

"Don't," I said. Coldly. Shakily. "Don't even try."

I couldn't even move. My feet felt nailed to the floor. The walls spun. The air thinned. "It's not what you think," she whispered, stepping closer.

I laughed. A sound that came out more like a sob. "Then please, *educate* me, Arohi. Because from what I *saw*, your tongue was down my best friend's throat while you were in *my* gift, in *my* memory."

"It just… happened," she tried again, voice breaking.

"You don't *accidentally* make out," I snapped. "Unless love's just another line you feed before unzipping someone else's jeans."

Mohak finally spoke. "Hriday, listen to me, man. It's not like that. I didn't plan this. I swear."

"But you didn't stop it either, did you?" I spat, the rage now boiling in me. "Was this your plan all along? pretending to be my brother while screwing my girl behind my back?"

He didn't respond.

Arohi's eyes were glassy now. "We never meant for it to happen this way. We never intended for it to go this far."

She broke down. "I didn't mean to hurt you."

"But you did." I took a step back, blinking away tears I didn't want to shed, not here, not now. "And you know what hurts the most? Not that you cheated. Not even that you did it with *him*."

I pointed at Mohak, who now looked like a shadow of himself. "It's that for even one second… I thought what we had was *real*."

The room fell into suffocating silence.

I turned to leave. I had nothing else to say, no more strength to stay where my heart had been ripped from my chest.

And as we walked off, I heard the muffled sounds of an argument behind me, her sobbing, Mohak cursing under his breath, the sound of something breaking.

But it didn't matter.

Something *had* broken. And this time, it was me.

Just as I turned to leave, trying to carry whatever shreds of self-respect I had left, I heard Madhav's voice cut through the air like a knife.

"*You're disgusting, Mohak.*"

His voice shook, not with fear, but fury. Mohak scoffed. "What's your problem now?"

Madhav stepped forward, eyes blazing. "*My problem?* You were supposed to be his brother! You've not just stabbed Hriday in the back, you twisted the knife and smiled while doing it."

Mohak's smirk disappeared. His jaw tightened.

"What's wrong?" he snapped, voice rising. "Why is everyone acting like I committed murder?"

I stopped.

My body turned before my mind could stop it. My fists clenched. My veins throbbed.

I was two seconds away from *punching him into the floor*, but that wasn't me. That had never been me.

Mohak looked straight into my eyes and suddenly *snapped.*

"Yeah, Hriday. Look at me. You want answers?"

He shouted, chest heaving with years of something dark and buried.

"*I was always the popular one.* Remember that? I was the guy everyone liked, the one girls crushed on, the one who walked into a room and *owned* it!"

My heart pounded like a war drum.

He kept going, unhinged. "And then YOU came. You with your fake soft-boy charm and deep poetry shit. Suddenly *you* became the captain. *You* got the teacher's praise, *you* led the basketball team. *You* got the crowd cheering your name."

He laughed bitterly.

"*And then* you got her. The prettiest girl. The one I thought might finally see *me.* But no, she saw *you.* Just like everyone else. All I got from being with you was becoming the background character in your story."

I swallowed hard, my chest burning. Golu stood frozen, fists tight, eyes wide.

Mohak stepped forward now, like a demon pulling off his mask.

"And let me make something clear," he hissed. "This wasn't the first time."

The room went silent. I blinked. "What...?"

He smirked. "Remember the day you were late for basketball practice? And you found Arohi outside the court?"

The blood in my body turned to ice.

"She was with me," he said slowly. "We were at *your* spot. The same place you took her later like it was some magical secret. But guess what, Bro? I had her there."

I turned to Arohi instinctively, hoping, begging for her to say something. To deny it. To slap him. To scream that he was lying.

But she just… stood there.

Silent.

Eyes down.

Not a word.

Even her guilt looked muted, like it had already made peace with the crime.

My eyes turned red. My throat was too tight to speak. The pain had surpassed heartbreak, it was now somewhere deeper, somewhere even words couldn't reach.

Golu stepped in.

He walked up and grabbed my hand, steady and strong. "*We're done here.* He's not worth one more second of your pain."

I didn't resist. I couldn't.

My body was there, but I was already somewhere else, sinking, drowning. As Golu pulled me out of the room, I heard Mohak's final dagger behind me.

"She's *mine* now, Hriday. She enjoys *more* with me. And deep down, you know it."

The door slammed behind us.

And with it, something inside me shattered so loudly… I wasn't sure if I'd ever hear peace again.

HRIDAY

I climbed the old stairs, one trembling step at a time. Each creak under my foot sounded like a scream inside my head. It was the same staircase... the same rusted railing... but nothing felt the same anymore.

The terrace.

It used to feel like magic up here. The breeze would always carry her perfume, and the stars felt closer when Arohi sat beside me, her head on my shoulder, whispering dreams into the night. We carved our names on the wall once. *Hriday & Arohi*, forever. I ran my fingers over that faint scribble today.

It's still here. But she isn't.

And neither is the boy who once stood by me like a shadow. Mohak, my best friend. My brother.

I used to believe in them more than I believed in myself. I never thought the two people I loved most could become the ones who tore me apart.

But they did.

They chose each other. Behind my back. While I was planning surprises, while I was writing love letters, while I was dreaming of a future with her and trusting *him* with every little secret of my heart, *they* were making memories of their own.

I laughed when I found out. That strange, broken kind of laugh that tastes like blood and salt. Because it couldn't be true, right?

But then I saw them.

Together. Holding hands. Whispering like we used to. Eyes locked in that shameless comfort I once thought belonged to me.

And it crushed me.

Now here I am, back at the terrace. The place where Arohi once told me she could see her entire future in my eyes.

What a joke.

There's an emptiness in the air tonight. Not the calm kind, the cruel kind. The kind that reminds you how silent everything becomes after heartbreak explodes inside you.

I sat down at our old spot. Back then, we used to count stars. Tonight, I only count regrets.

I remember the way her laughter used to echo here. God, I was stupid enough to believe that kind of happiness lasts.

And Mohak, he knew. He *knew* how much she meant to me. He was the one I ran to after every fight with her. He was the one who wiped my tears the first time she ignored my texts.

All the while… he was stealing her.

Not once did he blink when he hugged me, not once did she flinch when she called me *her love*, knowing she already gave her heart to someone else, *my someone else*.

I feel sick.

Betrayal doesn't stab. It seeps. Slowly. It seeps into your bones, into the way you breathe, into every memory you once called "beautiful".

And standing here now, on the very rooftop where I once thought I was the happiest man alive, I've never felt more alone.

Sometimes, I wish I could forget. Sometimes, I wish I could hate them.

But all I do is remember. And all I feel… is broken.

It was Golu who took the initiative. He spoke to the teachers, called our parents, and arranged everything so we could stay back in Mussoorie for just one more day after everyone else left.

I didn't want to stay. But I couldn't bear the thought of sitting on that bus, watching *them*, Arohi and Mohak, as if nothing ever happened. I was already shattered; seeing their faces would've crushed whatever little was left of me.

Arohi never came to explain. Not once. Not a word. She just disappeared into silence, like I was nothing more than a forgotten phase in her story.

The next morning, the rest of the group left for Delhi. I watched the buses leave from the window of our room, heart heavy, breath shallow.

It was just me and Golu now.

We booked our flights for the next day, but the idea of going back to Delhi haunted me. That city held everything I wanted to forget. Yet, staying back in Mussoorie felt no better. It was like standing between two burning houses and not knowing which one would kill me slower.

I was lost in between. A ghost in my own skin.

Golu… he never left my side. He gave me space, but never let me fall too far. He didn't say much, but he stayed. And sometimes, that's more powerful than words.

After a day, we returned to Delhi.

The moment I stepped off the plane, something inside me broke again. The air smelled the same, but nothing felt familiar. I was terrified to return to school. Stupid, broken me, still holding on to some dying hope that Arohi might text, might say *something*. But she never did.

"Just two more months," Golu kept saying, "and all of this will be over. We'll pass out, move on."

But I couldn't. I didn't.

School had become a graveyard of memories. Every corner echoed with moments we had shared, her laughter by the library steps, the stolen glances during morning assemblies, the late notes she slipped into my books. Even the silence screamed her name.

So I stopped going altogether.

Two entire months. I locked myself inside the four walls of my room. My world shrank to the size of my bed and the echo of her name in my head. I stopped looking in the mirror. I stopped recognising the person staring back when I did. I put on weight, lost my charm, my glow, my reason.

But every night, without fail, I'd lie on my back, stare at the ceiling, and remember her. Not the betrayal. Not the lies. Just… her. The girl who once promised me forever.

And that's what hurt the most.

She forgot me like a dream.

While I remembered her like a prayer.

Two Years Later

HRIDAY

Nothing much had changed in the last two years, except that I got more bearded, and the reality that I had made it into Delhi University.

But that night... That night still followed me like a shadow I couldn't outrun.

No matter how far I came, how much I tried to grow past it, I couldn't forget her. I had loved every inch of her, every word, every flaw, every silence. And I knew, deep down, I would never be able to love someone like that again. Maybe not at all.

Outwardly, I had learned to smile. Laugh at the right moments. Nod at life's routines. But inside? I was still broken glass held together by habit.

Only Maa truly saw through the mask. She never pried, never pushed. She just stood by me, like she always had. My anchor through every storm, her quiet presence steadier than words.

Now, my focus was my escape. College, books, and dreams yet to be lived. I had set my eyes on MICA for my MBA, its blend of creativity and communication called to the writer in me. I'd already begun my preparations. It gave me purpose. It gave the silence in my chest something to hold on to.

Reading and writing slowly stitched together pieces of me that heartbreak had torn apart. Maa always encouraged it. "Books will teach you what people won't," she used to say, and now I understood what she meant.

Golu had also cracked DU. He knew everything, held my worst days without judgement, and stood by me when the world felt too loud. He was the only one I truly confided in now.

And so here I am, twenty, scarred, still healing. Not fully okay. But no longer drowning either.

Just… breathing.

Just beginning again.

10 July 2023

It still haunted me,

The thought of running into Arohi someday.

What if she suddenly texted me back after all these years? What if I saw her in a crowd, unprepared?

Every day, a dull discomfort lingered beneath the surface, like an ache I had learned to live with.

After lectures today, I wandered down to Fakir Chand Bookstore, my quiet escape from reality. It had started drizzling a little and I hated it. I had become a regular now, spending hours between shelves lined with stories I could disappear into. The scent of old paper and soft whispers of turning pages had started to feel like home.

A group of girls stood at the entrance clicking pictures. I waited patiently, pretending to scroll through my phone, then slipped inside and started searching for the book on my list.

That's when I noticed a girl.

She stood in front of the shelf, indecisive, holding a copy of *Normal People*. She picked it up, put it back, then reached for it again, twice. I smiled softly and said, "Go for it. It's actually a good one."

She looked at me, a flicker of curiosity in her eyes, and smiled back.

"Okay, then. I will."

At the billing counter, she turned to me and asked,

"So... what's the best part about this one? Tell me without giving a spoiler."

I paused for a second, then smiled.

"'I don't think I'm a religious person... but *God made you for me.*' There's this line that hit the hardest."

She laughed, tossing her hair behind playfully.

"Woah. Why doesn't anyone ever say something like that to me?"

I smiled.

We stepped out together, books in hand. She flipped through the first few pages and frowned jokingly.

"290 pages?! Surely going to finish this today, also can you tell me something more about this one?"

I chuckled.

"You just imagine yourself as one of the characters. Live in the story. The more you read, the more you discover about yourself too."

She looked up, half-amused, half-soft.

"Let me guess… you had imaginary friends as a kid?"

"Had?" I raised my eyebrow, smirking. "I *still* have them."

She laughed again, gently, as if trying to memorise the moment.

"Books are magic, aren't they?" I said.

"For 100 pages, you're in another world… and in that world, you're always the best version of yourself."

"I think," she said softly, her eyes holding mine for a moment longer, "you might be the best version even in real life."

I didn't know what to say. So, I just smiled.

And as she turned left and I turned right, our paths briefly crossed.

It was just another morning.

The same alarm. The same silence.

The same heaviness that never really left.

Two years had passed, yet nothing felt different.

I woke up like I had every single day – quiet, tired and hollow.

Not a day went by without her name brushing against my thoughts like a memory I couldn't bury.

Arohi.

The tulips reminded me of her, the ones she loved, the ones I once filled our date with.

The metro rides echoed her laughter.

My Spotify playlists were mine, but the songs still belonged to her.

Even the coffee shop in the corner, where she never liked the coffee, reminded me of how she always came just for me.

Some memories don't fade.

They just sit quietly inside you and breathe.

By the time I reached college, I had rehearsed enough of my silences.

Golu was already waiting at the gate, his face brighter than mine would ever be again.

We walked in, same corridors, same class, until the moment wasn't. Someone was sitting at our usual bench.

I was about to turn away when Golu, being Golu, walked straight up to her. "Hey? Don't you know this is my bench?" he asked, casually but with a smirk.

She looked up slowly, pen still in hand, and for a second, time did something strange.

It was *her*.

The same girl I saw a few days back at Faqir Chand Bookstore.

She had that same smile, soft, almost teasing, framed by untamed hair falling on her round face.

She wore an oversized t-shirt tucked slightly into straight blue denims, paired with bold red dunks that didn't match the weather but somehow suited her anyway.

She blinked up at me, her voice almost playful. "You?"

Then smiled wider. "Hi… *Imaginary boy*."

Golu turned to me with a raised brow. "You know her?"

"No, I don't," I said flatly.

She chuckled and tilted her head, "We met at the bookstore, remember?"

"I do," I said, eyes fixed on the floor. "We don't really *know* each other."

I didn't mean to sound cold, but something in me, or maybe everything, had changed.

She lowered her voice just enough to shift the tone. "Hi. I'm Veda. Veda Sharma. I'm new here."

Then she glanced at Golu with a small smile. "Sorry about the seat. I didn't know it was taken."

To my absolute disbelief, Golu's tone melted into sudden warmth.

"No, no, it's fine, Veda. Please, it's yours now. Nice to meet you. I'm Madhav, but call me Golu. And that," he pointed towards me with a grin, "is Hriday. My best friend."

I just nodded, lips barely moving.

Then Golu asked the question lingering in both our minds, "But... who joins a new college in the final year?"

She smiled again, that smile like she's always been on her own side of the storm. "A seat opened up. I always wanted to get into DU. I mean, who doesn't, right? The campus, the culture, the air, everything here just feels... positive."

I couldn't help myself.

"It's all fake," I muttered, and pulled Golu away to the other bench.

The lectures dragged on, predictable and dull, just like every other day. Nothing sparked any excitement. As we stepped out, Golu nudged me, his voice low. "Veda's alone, Bhai. Should we ask her to join us?"

I shook my head gently. "No need, Golu. She can handle herself. She seems sharp, like someone who'll make friends easily."

Golu glanced around. "Doesn't look like anyone's making the first move. Not even her."

Before I could respond, her voice broke through the hum of the crowd.

"Hey, where are you guys headed? Mind if I join?" Veda asked, her tone casual but hopeful.

"Yes! Of course, why not?" Golu replied quickly, flashing a grin. "In fact, Hriday was just about to ask you out."

I shot him a glare, but he only smirked.

"How about a cappuccino at Nescafé? It's the best coffee on campus," Golu offered. She nodded, her eyes lighting up. "Sounds perfect."

As we walked, I slung my backpack onto the bench. "You guys go ahead. I've got some write-ups to finish," I said, turning away.

But just then, I heard her soft voice trail behind me. "Okay, I'll skip it too. Maybe another time," Veda said as if she knew I avoided catching up. And just like that, she turned and began to walk away.

A pang of regret hit me, I had been too closed off, too distant. Maybe even cold.

"Hey, Veda!" I called out, my voice a little more urgent than I meant. "Let's go. We can always work later, if that's okay with you?"

She paused, then turned with a smile that said more than words ever could. "Sure."

We made our way to Nescafé. Golu went to place the order, leaving us alone for a moment. Silence hung between us, not awkward, but not quite comfortable either. She looked around, her eyes scanning the campus with quiet admiration.

She smiled faintly, the kind of smile people wear when they're living a dream they once whispered to themselves. Maybe this place, this university, meant more to her than she let on.

When Golu returned, he broke the silence with his usual charm. "So, Veda," he said, placing the tray down, "tell us about yourself."

VEDA

"So, you guys finally know my name," I said with a smile. "I'm Veda Sharma."

There's always something about introducing yourself that feels like opening a little window into your world. And mine? It's been a journey.

"I'm from Indore. Spent all of my 20 years there, growing up, dreaming big, and always looking beyond the horizon. I always wanted to be here, at DU. Missed it by just one mark. One single mark." I paused, letting out a soft laugh. "But I've always believed in destiny. Somehow, I just knew life would find a way to bring me here."

I looked around, the campus buzzing with life, and I knew, I was exactly where I was meant to be.

"And here I am now... living the life I once dreamed of, right down to the little details."

It's been ten days since I moved to Delhi, and honestly? I'm already crushing on this city. Every lane, every sunset, every corner café feels like a page from a story I always wanted to live. I've walked through Khan Market, roamed around Majnu Ka Tilla, gotten lost in Chandni Chowk's chaos, watched the sun dip behind India Gate... all the places I had only seen in photos. And now, they're part of my every day.

These little things, they make me the happiest.

I live with two of my school friends in Lajpat Nagar. They've been in Delhi for the last three years, and we now share a small apartment full of laughter, midnight Maggi, and way too many stories.

And today, just maybe, I get to make two more friends.

MADHAV

"Whoa! That was quite the introduction," I said, laughing as I placed my empty cup on the table. "My cappuccino's already over. You better finish yours while we take turns telling you about us."

Veda chuckled, her eyes twinkling. "And yes," I added with a grin, "you're definitely getting two new friends today."

Hriday just sat there, a little lost, clearly not catching the undertone.

I leaned in. "So, I'm Madhav, but people close to me call me Golu. You can too," I said with a wink. "And this guy here," I added, patting Hriday's back, "is my best friend. We've been inseparable since we were two."

"Since *two*?" Veda's jaw dropped slightly, her smile widening in surprise.

"Yup!" I said proudly, throwing a little playful flex for effect.

Veda turned to Hriday then, her tone softening. "And you? Tell me something about yourself."

He hesitated for a second, then spoke gently. "There's not much to say."

Veda didn't press. She just smiled quietly, looking down at her cappuccino, letting the silence speak for itself.

"It was really nice meeting you, Veda. Friends?" I asked, holding out my hand. She flashed her widest smile and replied, "Yes, friends!" We shook hands, and I nudged

Hriday to do the same. He did, though without much enthusiasm.

HRIDAY

"Hriday, Professor Sekhar told me I could ask you for help with my assignments. Would you mind?" Veda asked softly.

Her voice stirred something in me, a memory.

Arohi had once asked me the same thing, and I remember how thrilled I was back then. That moment, that feeling, came rushing back like a wave. For a second, I was lost in that flashback, her smile, her voice, everything.

Veda waved her hand in front of my face, bringing me back to the present.

"Am I supposed to help everyone who joins mid-session?" I snapped, my tone harsher than I intended. "I've got my own work. Sorry, I can't."

Her smile faded in an instant, the brightness in her eyes dimming. Golu looked at me, stunned, not saying a word.

Without responding, Veda quietly stood up and walked away.

"Hriday, is this really how you talk to someone?" Golu's voice broke the silence between us. "What's got into you? I know you've changed, but don't turn yourself into someone so cold. Not everyone's the same, Hriday. She just asked for a little help."

He paused, then added more softly, "I get that it's not easy… but it's not that hard to be kind either."

Golu rarely spoke like this, but when he did, it struck deep.

"You know, I could've chosen anyone to be our friend," he continued, "but there's something about Veda. She's got this rare kind of charm, a quiet positivity that's hard to ignore. Maybe it's too soon to say anything, but I don't think I'm wrong. She's different, her smile, that warmth she carries, it's rare these days. She lights up a room without even trying."

With that, Golu gave me a lingering look, then stood up and walked away, leaving me to sit with everything he'd just said.

The guilt sat heavy in my chest.

How much had I changed… for someone who never truly cared?

I walked into class, lost in thought, and my eyes instantly found her, Veda, sitting quietly on the last bench, tucked into a corner with the same book she had picked up with me the other day.

But this time, I really saw her.

Her straight, bouncy hair shimmered like something out of a shampoo commercial, catching the light with every movement. Her face, soft, round, and glowing with a wheatish warmth, made her look effortlessly adorable. A stubborn strand of hair kept falling over her eyes, and she kept tucking it behind her ear with the sweetest kind of annoyance.

She wore a simple red t-shirt, paired with black denims and a different pair of dunks today, yet she looked... magnetic. Golu was right. There was something about her, an energy, a charm, that drew you in without asking for it.

I walked up to her, notebook in hand.

"Here you go, Veda," I said quietly. "I'm sorry... for earlier."

She looked up, smiled gently, and took the notebook from me.

"I understand, Hriday," she said, her voice steady and kind. "Not everything needs a reason, Hriday. Some things just take time. And that's okay."

And then, with a playful grin, she added, "Dosti mein no sorry, no thank you."

We both laughed.

"So you're filmy too?" I teased.

She smiled wider this time, and for the first time in a while, something inside me softened.

VEDA

After classes, I headed home and got straight to work. I had to pick up my pace if I wanted to match the rest of the class. Slipping into my comfiest pajamas, I tied up my hair in a loose bun and sat down with Hriday's notebook.

The moment I opened it, I blinked in surprise.

Wait… do boys actually have such neat handwriting?

I couldn't help but smile to myself, it looked like a string of tiny pearls, flowing effortlessly across the page.

As I began copying the notes, I found myself pausing every now and then, especially when I reached the last few pages. They were filled with random scribbles, scattered thoughts, and quotes that carried a strange weight. Some were vague, others piercing. But all of them… felt personal.

There was something oddly captivating about it, like reading the margins of someone's unspoken world. And I won't lie, it made the study session a little more interesting than I'd expected.

It was a slow, golden Saturday morning when Anika and Sivi, my closest friends and roommates, asked if I wanted to tag along to a friend's house party.

But parties were never really *me*.

As an only child, I'd grown to cherish my solitude. I found comfort in quiet corners, in moments shared with people who *truly* mattered, or sometimes, with just myself. There was something peaceful about my own company, about simply being still in a world that never stopped spinning.

So, with a gentle smile, I told them I'd pass.

I already had a day planned, one I'd been looking forward to. First, a visit to Faqir Chand, my little haven of stories and stillness, where time seemed to pause between bookshelves. And then, I'd head to L'Opéra in Connaught Place, a place that had quietly become my favourite. Their desserts? A slice of happiness I never said no to.

Sometimes, the perfect day is the one you spend with yourself, and everything that quietly makes your heart full.

The next morning, I returned Hriday's notebook and thanked him.

He simply smiled in response, no words, just that quiet, unreadable smile.

By now, Golu and I had grown pretty close. He was fun, easy to talk to, and our bond had naturally settled into this playful, brother-sister dynamic. But with Hriday, it was different. There was a distance I couldn't bridge, not because I didn't want to, but because he seemed so guarded, like he belonged to a world tucked somewhere far inside himself.

Still, I never pushed.

Some connections take time, and I respected that.

Golu and Hriday were the only people I really knew here at DU, and after classes that day, I decided to head to Khan Market for a little walk and some fresh air.

It had begun to drizzle, the kind of soft, silver rain that made July feel like poetry. There's something magical about rain… it doesn't ask questions, it doesn't rush. It just falls, washing away everything loud, leaving behind silence and the scent of beginnings.

I stepped into Faqir Chand, my go-to escape, and there he was, Hriday, already there, skimming through shelves with focused eyes.

Without thinking too much, I walked over and tapped him gently on the shoulder. "Hey…"

He turned, a bit surprised at first. "Oh, Veda. You again?"

I grinned. "What, am I not allowed here?"

"No, no, just surprised you came," he said, this time with a real smile.

It was the first time he spoke to me so casually, without that wall around his words. "So… you come here every day?" I asked, curious.

"Saturdays are for Faqir Chand," he replied, almost like a ritual.

Something about the way he said it – soft, honest – stayed with me. And in that tiny exchange, something shifted.

Maybe not much, but enough to feel it.

HRIDAY

At Faqir Chand today, I ran into Veda again.

She wore a black chikankari kurti paired with baggy jeans, simple, yet striking. A small bindi adorned her forehead, and her jhumkas danced gently with every step she took.

"Is black your favourite colour?" I asked, half-smiling.

She gave me one of her signature dramatic expressions. "How do *you* know that?"

I chuckled. "It's been almost a month since we met, Veda. And in all this time, I've seen you wear black in more variations than I can count."

With a playful wink, she replied, "Life is already so colourful, I prefer dressing in black. Besides, I think it makes me look calmer."

I laughed. "You're such a cutie, Veda."

The words slipped out before I could stop them. Her cheeks turned the faintest shade of pink, and instantly, I regretted saying it.

I awkwardly gathered my books and said a quick goodbye before heading out of the store.

The rain had started by then, steady and soft, so I took shelter under a nearby bus stop. Moments later, I saw her again, running through the rain towards the same spot.

She looked... carefree. Her arms slightly out, her smile wide. I'd never seen anyone enjoy the rain like that.

"You again?" she said, breathless but glowing. I just nodded.

"I love the rain," she said, looking up at the sky. "It's so dreamy."

"What's so dreamy about getting drenched?" I muttered. "Feels more like a waste of time."

"You find everything a waste," she replied, rolling her eyes.

I turned my face away, pretending I didn't hear the quiet disappointment in her voice.

"Are you free?" she asked after a pause.

"Why?"

"Let's grab some desserts at L'Opéra. My treat. I *love* that place."

The name hit me like a wave. L'Opéra.

Ours. Mine and Arohi's. We'd spent nearly all our dates there. Since she left... I hadn't stepped foot in that place. Not once.

"Look, Veda," I said flatly. "I don't have time to waste on café hopping. Especially not in the rain. You go ahead."

And with that, I walked away.

A few steps later, something made me turn around. She wasn't at the bus stop anymore.

I don't know what came over me when I spoke like that. All I know is, it didn't feel good. Not at all. Not when it came to her.

"I never mean to talk to her like that, Golu..." I said, my voice low, carrying more guilt than I could admit. "But I end up doing it anyway. Every single time. She's too genuine, too kind, and yet I say things she never deserves to hear. And the strangest part? She still comes back. With the same calm charm in her eyes. As if I hadn't hurt her. As if nothing ever happened."

Golu looked at me, thoughtfully, before placing a hand on my shoulder.

"That's because she's rare, Hriday. Veda sees something real in you. I've spent a good amount of time with her now... she doesn't think you hurt her on purpose. She never takes it that way. And honestly, I don't think you ever do either. She told me once, 'There's something about Hriday... something that feels unreal. Like he's holding back a storm.'"

Hearing that broke something inside me. A silence fell between us, only filled by the sound of my thoughts.

Tears blurred my vision. "You know, Golu... I see just a part of Arohi in her. Just a flicker. The way she looks at me sometimes, those eyes, they remind me of when Arohi used to look at me like I was her whole world. Veda doesn't even know, but she brings those memories back without trying."

Golu exhaled, nodding slowly. "I get you, Bhai. Not everyone's the same, and maybe that's the point. You don't have to fake a thing. Just be yourself. Maybe you two are just meant to be good friends, and that's okay."

Just then, a notification popped up on our WhatsApp group, Third Wheeling, the one Veda, Golu and I shared.

Veda: *Boys, I'm baking brownies for us!*

I saw Golu immediately spam the chat with those "yummy" emojis. I smiled faintly, but inside… I drifted back.

Back to the day Arohi gave me a little box tied with a ribbon. A sticker on top that said, *"I bake for the special ones."* I had held on to that box like it was a secret confession, like maybe, just maybe, she had started feeling the same.

But now, with Veda, every little thing she did pulled me into my past. Unknowingly, unintentionally… yet deeply.

And despite everything, something about her presence still lingers in the quiet corners of my heart. I didn't say a word, but the silence was loud. There was something about Veda that unsettled me, not in fear, but in memory.

MADHAV

The scent of freshly baked brownies lingered in the air, warm and tempting, like a hug in sugar form. I was mid-chew, attempting to take what was probably the most *disrespectfully large* bite of Veda's masterpiece, when I finally managed to speak, mouth half-full, eyes wide with delight.

"Guys," I mumbled, chocolate practically oozing from the corner of my lips, "how about a house party tonight? My place. Just the three of us."

Veda raised an eyebrow, suspicious. Hriday sipped on his coffee silently, as always. "Wait, your parents?" Veda asked.

"Gone!" I said, dramatically throwing my arms in the air. "Haridwar! With the grandparents! I am home alone. It's basically a crime *not* to throw a party."

Veda clapped her hands. "Sounds great! I'll cook pasta for us!"

I blinked at her. "There it is. You and your undying love for cooking." I gave her an exaggerated eye-roll, the kind worthy of an Oscar.

She pouted. "I want to, Golu. Pleaseee."

Cue: puppy eyes, head tilt, tiny whine. Classic.

"You're dangerously good at emotional blackmail," I said, pointing a finger at her while pretending to squint. "Fine. But if the pasta sucks, we're ordering pizza and never letting you touch garlic again."

She grinned like a villain in a cooking show. "Deal."

I turned to Hriday. "And you, Sir? Are we graced with your majestic presence tonight?"

Hriday, still chewing his brownie like he was tasting a memory, simply said, "Yes, yes. I'll come up."

I gasped. "What?! That was the fastest yes I've ever heard from you. Veda, he didn't even do his usual 'let me check my mood and the weather and my birth chart' routine!"

Veda laughed. "Maybe it's the brownie talking." Hriday shrugged. "Or maybe I just like pasta." We all burst into laughter.

HRIDAY

The doorbell rang just as I was finishing an attempt at setting up fairy lights in Golu's living room.

I opened the door and there she was.

She wore a black mini dress tonight, simple, yet it hugged her in all the right ways, making her look effortlessly stunning. Her hair was curled to soft perfection, cascading down her shoulders like waves that knew exactly where to fall. She was glowing, radiant in that quiet, unbothered way that couldn't be faked.

Tiny bow studs peeked from beneath her curls, delicate and sweet, like something out of a vintage film. She'd done just the bare minimum with makeup, a whisper of winged liner, barely-there gloss, and still, she looked like she'd walked out of a dream.

"Can I come in, or are you planning to keep staring at me like that?" she asked, smirking, one eyebrow raised.

I looked away, pretending to fix my sleeves. "Just checking if you brought the pasta."

"Priorities," she muttered, brushing past me.

We kicked off the night with old songs playing on the speaker, the three of us dancing terribly in the kitchen as Veda took charge like she was on *MasterChef: Chaotic Edition*. She threatened us with a wooden spoon whenever we tried to sneak a taste, while I quietly grated cheese with what could only be described as... precision passion.

Dinner was a blur of laughter, overcooked garlic bread, and far too much cheese.

After stuffing ourselves, Golu leaned back on the couch and smirked. "Guys... you know what this calls for?"

I raised an eyebrow. "Please don't say karaoke."

He pointed dramatically towards the bar cabinet in the corner. "My dad's sacred stash. The Hidden Temple."

Veda's eyes widened. "No, no, no! Your mom will kill you. You're not even allowed to breathe near that bar."

"That's why we'll drink it in silent respect," Golu said solemnly. "One shot. To pasta. To friendship. To forbidden things."

Veda groaned, hands on her hips. "This is a bad idea."

I, already halfway to the cabinet, shrugged. "Most fun things are." We clinked glasses and downed the shot.

Three seconds later, Golu was on the floor. Like, *on the floor*.

"I think I saw my soul leave," Golu whispered dramatically, hand over my chest.

Veda burst out laughing. "Golu, you're *one shot* down and already giving Oscar-worthy monologues."

"I'm fine," golu mumbled. "The floor is just... emotionally supportive right now." I chuckled, *actually chuckled*, and helped me to the couch.

Veda handed me water, muttering, "Children. I'm surrounded by children."

VEDA

Hriday poured himself another glass of Jack Daniel's, his hand a little too loose on the bottle now. He looked over at me, blinking slowly, a lazy smile playing on his lips.

"Why aren't you having any?" he asked, slurring slightly.

"I don't like the stuff," I replied, tucking my knees closer to my chest on the sofa.

Hriday, by now, was completely gone, his eyes glassy, voice unsteady, and his usual control lost somewhere between the third and fourth pour. Without warning, he grabbed my wrist gently and pulled me up.

"Come," he mumbled.

I didn't resist, though I wasn't sure why. He led me to the balcony. I'd begged Golu and Hriday to decorate with fairy lights. And they had. Little golden stars dangled and blinked softly all around us, glowing against the night.

Golu lay passed out on the floor inside, utterly unaware of the world around him. Typical.

Hriday made me sit beside him, our knees brushing slightly. He stared out into the night, a faint breeze tousling his hair.

"You should lie down," I said gently. "You're too drunk, Hriday."

He turned to me, his eyes hazy but holding something heartbreakingly honest. "Listen, Miss Veda, no, wait... Miss Cutie," he grinned, clearly lost in his own world. "You know you're absolutely... *cutie*. And you remind me of Arohi. You really do."

My breath caught, but I said nothing.

"She had the same eyes. The same way of looking at me... like I was enough." His voice cracked on the last word.

"I loved her so much," he whispered. "I was ready to marry her someday. She was my world. My person. Everything I had ever imagined for my future was with her. And one day, it all just... disappeared."

He leaned back against the railing, voice low and trembling now.

"She cheated. With my best friend. Mohak. Can you believe that?" He laughed bitterly, shaking his head. "I lost them both. In one day. Just like that."

There was nothing playful left in him now. He looked hollow, like someone who hadn't slept in years.

"I don't know if I'll ever be able to love again, Veda," he said. "I don't even know who I am without her. Every part of me still aches. Still hopes she'll come back. Isn't that pathetic?"

"No," I said quietly. "It's not."

"I see her in you, sometimes. You look at me the same way she did. And it scares me."

His voice broke then, and for a moment, I saw the boy behind all that silence. The one who never really stopped bleeding.

"Everything will be alright, Hriday," I said softly, brushing a hand across his arm. "Come on, you need to lie down."

He stumbled as he stood, and instinctively, I caught him. All of him. His full 5'8 frame practically collapsed into mine, and I, barely 5'3, nearly lost balance trying to keep us both upright.

"You're heavy, you idiot," I muttered under my breath, steadying him.

He mumbled something incoherent, probably another version of "cutie", and leaned on me completely as I guided him toward Golu's room. I tucked him under the covers like a child, brushing his hair back once out of instinct, before pulling the blanket over him.

For a long second, I just stood there, watching him sleep. There was something painfully beautiful about how peaceful he looked, even if only because he was too drunk to remember the pain.

I tiptoed out quietly and walked back to the balcony. The night had settled now, soft, still, and heavy with things unsaid. I sat under the fairy lights, alone, wrapped in silence and thoughts that felt too loud inside me.

And somewhere between the glow of the lights and the shadows in my heart, I realised, this boy hadn't healed. He hadn't even begun. And somehow, without meaning to, I had walked right into the middle of his storm.

He once told me I reminded him of his past, but I knew I had to become his strength, the one who helps him face it, not flee from it. It's always better to confront what life throws at you than to keep running. And I had to make him see that.

I went back to check on the boys. They were fast asleep, peacefully, like children lost in dreams. As I glanced around, I noticed Hriday's backpack lying open on the floor. I bent down to pick it up and place it on the chair, when a few things spilled out. I gathered them gently, and among them was a polaroid, of Hriday and, I assumed, Arohi.

It was perfect, almost heartbreakingly so. They looked genuinely happy. She was stunning, and Hriday... I had never seen him that radiant. He was kissing her cheek with such intensity, and her eyes were closed as if she was lost in the warmth of that moment. They held each other like the world didn't exist beyond them. It made me feel a twinge of jealousy, but strangely, it also made me smile. To see him like that, in love, glowing, alive.

I placed the photo back in his bag and returned to the drawing room, curling up on the sofa. But that picture lingered in my thoughts. All I could think about was how deeply I wanted to see Hriday smile like that again. He deserved that kind of happiness. He deserved the world.

And yes, I liked him, probably more than I'd ever admit. But some feelings, you learn to carry quietly.

HRIDAY

"Good morning, boys," Veda's voice rang softly through the room. She stood at the entrance with a tray in hand, a gentle smile playing on her lips. "Here's something to help you battle that hangover. You guys were absolutely insane last night."

I sat up slowly, only to see Golu sprawled across the floor, clutching his head dramatically.

"What is this pain? I swear my brain's about to explode," he groaned.

"No one told you to drink like it was a competition," Veda said, raising her voice a notch.

"How on earth did I end up on the bed?" I asked, genuinely puzzled. "I carried you," she replied. "And you're a lot heavier than you look."

"And Golu?"

She chuckled. "Sorry, I didn't have the strength left to lift him too."

To which Golu mumbled, "It's okay, the floor and I had a heart-to-heart last night. We're emotionally attached now."

We laughed as we took the drinks she handed us. They were oddly refreshing. "I made some breakfast too," Veda said, setting the tray down. "But I'll head out now, Golu."

"Nooo, stay! It's Saturday, let's skip college today," Golu pleaded, puppy eyes in full swing.

"Actually, that sounds like a great idea," Hriday joined in. "I could use a break too."

"I've got some errands. I go to Faqir Chand every Saturday after class," she replied, glancing at the clock.

"We could go together then," I offered quickly. "And besides, we need more of your meals in our lives." I threw her a playful wink.

Her face lit up instantly, Veda always glowed a little more when someone appreciated her cooking. And just like that, she agreed to stay.

Breakfast was simple but perfect, sandwiches that somehow tasted like comfort and warmth. Golu devoured fifteen without blinking. Veda didn't complain once. She just sat there, feeding us with that same peaceful, happy smile.

We had shared everything, our childhood stories, our silly crushes, our heartbreaks. It felt effortless, like peeling away layers until there was nothing left to hide. Then came a silence, not awkward, but still, like the air paused to listen.

Veda broke it gently. "You know… I'm my parents' only child," she said, her voice softening. "Growing up, everything felt magical. Like I was living in a dream. I was loved fiercely, purely. My parents' love wasn't just for me or for each other; it radiated in all directions, a perfect , unbroken circle that held the three of us together. They were best friends… the kind you only see in old movies."

"Were?" Golu interrupted, confused.

She nodded. "Yes… they left me two years ago. A car accident. It was sudden." The room fell into a heavy silence, like time itself was mourning with us. I looked at her, stunned, trying to find the right words, but none seemed worthy.

"I miss them every single day," she continued, her eyes glistening but her voice steady. "Of course I do. How could I not? They were my whole world. But I also know... they never really left me. I carry them with me, in everything I do, in every moment I choose to keep going."

She smiled faintly through the ache, the kind of smile that only comes from knowing deep loss. "My mother used to tell me, 'You don't wait for life to be perfect to be grateful. You find happiness in the small, even when everything feels broken.' She taught me to laugh on days

I could barely breathe. To see light when I felt lost. To say thank you, even when it hurt."

We listened, quiet, moved, raw.

"Pain doesn't go away. It just becomes part of you," she said, looking at me now. "But our lives... they are far too precious to stop living because of someone who broke us. People will hurt us, leave us, abandon us, but we cannot abandon ourselves."

Her words hit something deep inside me, like they were stitched with a truth I hadn't dared to face yet. She wiped a tear that had quietly escaped down her cheek, not out of weakness, but as if making space for strength to settle in its place.

Veda chose to live with grace, to find joy in the wreckage, and to love what remained. And in that moment, she wasn't just the strongest person in the room, she was also the brightest.

After an hour, Veda and I got ready for the book hunt, while Golu called up his close friend, soon to be his girlfriend. She was exactly like Golu: chubby, cheerful, and always thinking about food.

I waited in the drawing room, aimlessly scrolling through my phone, when I saw Veda step out of the guest room.

For a moment, everything around me seemed to freeze. There she was, looking like a perfectly unfinished poem. She had chosen her usual oversized t-shirt, but today it was a deep green one with "Manhattan" written across it, almost as if it hinted at some distant dream she carried in her heart. The shirt loosely draped over her frame, paired with her ripped jeans that revealed the careless yet effortless edges of her personality.

She wore chunky black glasses that slightly covered her cheeks, the same cheeks that turned pink when she laughed too hard. Her hair was loosely clipped, small strands falling around her face like they were meant to be there, softly rebellious. I knew her, she would probably open them and let them flow freely once we reached the bookstore, pretending she didn't care but secretly knowing how beautiful she looked that way.

As I watched her adjusting the clip, tucking a few strands behind her ear, something inside me shifted quietly. It felt like standing at the edge of a cliff, knowing you could fall but not daring to move forward.

I wasn't ready to admit it, not even to myself, but somewhere beneath my guarded silences and casual jokes, I was falling for her. Slowly, helplessly. And yet, I kept telling myself I wasn't. I couldn't.

"I'm ready, Hriday. Shall we go?" she asked, her voice breaking softly through my thoughts. I just chose to nod, words somehow felt too heavy to form.

"Golu, lock the door. We're leaving," Veda called out.

Golu came running from the kitchen, excitement and nervousness painted all over his face. He was busy preparing lunch for Sia, the girl he hoped would soon be more than just a friend.

"Guys, wish me luck," he said, his voice trembling with a rare vulnerability. Veda and I exchanged a quick look before we pulled him into a warm hug.

"They'd better get along this time," Veda whispered as we stepped into the lift, her eyes lingering with a hint of worry and hope. "I really wish she's the one for Golu."

I pressed the button for the ground floor and turned to her, managing only a quiet "yes". The word felt small, almost swallowed by the gentle closeness that settled between us in that moment, a closeness neither of us dared to name yet.

VEDA

The lift smelled faintly like a bakery, all thanks to Hriday. We stood apart, leaning against opposite doors, a distance that felt both awkward and electric. Hriday stood there with his arms folded across his chest, a silent guard to his own thoughts.

I couldn't stop stealing glances at him. He wore a crisp white shirt tucked into faded blue jeans, paired effortlessly with his Nikes. His hair was perfectly groomed, each strand in place, and his glasses looked as if they had been crafted just for him, framing his face in a way that made it almost impossible to look away.

When we stepped out of the lift, I unclipped my hair, letting it tumble down my shoulders.

"I knew you'd do that," Hriday said, a teasing edge in his voice.

"Liar," I shot back, half-smiling. "How could you possibly know what I was going to do?"

"Arohi used to do the same," he replied before he could stop himself. The words seemed to hang in the air, sharp and fragile. I saw the colour drain from his face instantly.

"It's okay, Hriday," I said softly, trying to ease the sudden heaviness. "Most girls do that. It's nothing unusual. Let's go."

We reached the subway and arrived at Khan Market in no time. As we stepped out of the metro station, the scent of fresh flowers drifted towards us from a florist's shop nearby.

"Don't you like flowers?" Hriday asked, his voice gentle.

"Yes!" I replied, my face lighting up. "I love sunflowers."

"Same, Veda," he said, and for the first time, I saw a genuine, carefree smile spread across his face, the kind that starts in the eyes and spills over like sunlight.

The florist recognised him immediately. "Bhaiya, where have you been? It's been so long! Should I pack some tulips for you? They're fresh today."

"Not today," Hriday replied, his tone clipped, and we quickly walked away. In that moment, I understood, tulips must have been her favourite.

As we strolled towards the bookstore, I turned to him and said, "You know, Hriday, if I ever find my person, whoever he might be, I won't ask him to buy me flowers. Instead, I'd want him to shake a tree for me, so that when I stand beneath it, all the flowers fall around me. That's what Papa used to do for Maa, and that's what I dream of too."

"I want the kind of love where letters meant more than texts. Where holding hands felt like a promise.

Where love wasn't rushed… it grew, like roots beneath the surface before it ever bloomed."

"I like love that stays. Love that waits. Love that knows silence can still mean understanding. Someone who sees me on the days I don't know how to be seen. I would always and always want my story to be an old-school one." I glanced at him finally.

"Someone who doesn't run when things get quiet."

Hriday looked at me, a soft, almost wistful smile playing on his lips. And without saying a word, we stepped into the bookstore together, as if crossing into a quiet world only we knew.

As soon as we stepped out of the store, we were greeted by a downpour so heavy it felt like the whole sky had decided to fall at once. The bookstore was too crowded for us to go back to it, and thankfully, I had my umbrella with me.

I quickly opened it, and we both squeezed underneath it. Hriday struggled to fit in at first, awkwardly bumping against me, until he finally pulled me closer by my shoulders and took hold of the umbrella himself. Half of me ended up pressed against him, I could feel the warmth of his body, the quiet thump of his heartbeat so close that it made my own heart stutter.

"Why is it always raining whenever we come here?" Hriday muttered, sounding half frustrated, half amused.

"I love it, though," I replied with a soft smile, tilting my face up to catch a few stray droplets.

"Oh? What is it that you don't like, then?" he teased, pulling at my cheek gently, his fingers lingering a little longer than they should have. My laughter got caught somewhere in my throat. In that fleeting second, the world around us disappeared, it was just me, him, and the rain drumming its own secret song above our heads.

"Let's stop by a café," Hriday suggested.

"No… let's go to that tea stall," I said, pointing at a tiny, almost hidden stall nearby. It looked humble, with barely any space to sit, but it had a charm that called to me.

Hriday chuckled and nodded. "Fine, as you say."

We ordered two chai and a bun maska. The old vendor nodded warmly as Hriday placed the order. We sat on a semi-wet wooden bench, our knees brushing, the rain creating a blurry watercolour world around us.

I turned to look at him just as he was wiping his glasses, his hair damp and falling slightly over his forehead. In that unguarded moment, he looked so boyish, almost delicate, my heart did a little flip I tried to ignore.

He suddenly caught me staring, and instead of some cute line, he narrowed his eyes and said, "What?"

"Nothing!" I shot back, more flustered than I meant to be, folding my arms in a half-pout.

He laughed, a real, full laugh that melted into the rain-soaked evening, and I knew then that some moments aren't meant to be explained. They're meant to be felt.

We sat side by side on that small, damp bench, our hands wrapped around steaming clay cups of chai. The rain kept drumming steadily on the tin roof above, a soft music that felt like it belonged only to us. Every now and then, a gust of wind would blow droplets onto our faces, and we would both laugh, too loudly, too freely, as if we had forgotten the rest of the world.

Hriday dipped his bun maska into his tea with so much focus that it almost made me giggle. A little dollop of butter stuck to his lip, and without thinking, I reached out and wiped it away with my thumb. For a heartbeat, he froze. Our eyes locked, his breath hitched slightly, but then, almost immediately, he looked away, pretending to focus on his tea.

"Careful. You'll spill it all over yourself," I teased, trying to hide the tiny storm raging inside me.

"And then you'll be the one to clean it up, right?" he shot back, smirking, but there was a warmth behind his glasses that gave him away.

We finished our tea with quiet bursts of laughter, our shoulders brushing every now and then. Every touch felt like a tiny electric spark, but we both kept pretending it meant nothing.

Later, we decided to take a slow walk back, the rain now reduced to a gentle drizzle. We shared the umbrella again, our steps deliberately unhurried, as though we both secretly wished to make the moment last forever. I watched as he absentmindedly kicked tiny puddles along the path, his hair now completely messy and clinging to his forehead.

"Look at you, ruining your shoes," I scolded lightly.

"Better than you ruining your hair," he teased, flicking a wet strand away from my face. His fingers hovered a moment too long near my cheek before he pulled them back, clearing his throat awkwardly.

When we finally reached the main road, we both stood there, neither of us moving, as if we had arrived at an invisible line neither dared to cross.

"Well… this was fun," he said, pushing up his glasses.

"Yeah… just… friends hanging out," I replied, forcing a bright smile.

"Exactly. Just friends," he echoed, but the way his eyes lingered on me, the way my heart skipped, we both knew it was a lie.

But for now, it was easier to stay on our side of that line, holding on to our little secret feelings that we pretended didn't exist, while silently hoping one day, one of us would be brave enough to say it out loud.

HRIDAY

"I'll leave for my place now. Hriday," Veda teased, her eyes sparkling mischievously. "I have so much to do… all by myself."

"Let me drop you," I offered immediately.

"Oh! It's alright. I can escort myself," she laughed, waving her hand dismissively.

"Veda, come on. Let me drop you. It's alright," I insisted, my voice softer than I intended.

After two quick metro changes and a short walk through narrow lanes washed clean by the rain, we finally reached her apartment, a warm, welcoming building in Green Park.

"Okay… bye then," I said, hesitating at the gate.

"No way," she grinned, pulling me lightly by the arm. "It's your first time here, and I'm not letting you go without coming upstairs. Let's have Maggi."

"Okay," I agreed, though the truth was, I wanted to spend more time with her too, more than I could admit, even to myself.

As I stepped inside her apartment, a luxurious yet calming scent, almost like walking into a Marriott lobby, surrounded me. The space was immaculately clean, airy, and surprisingly huge for Delhi. Soft beige curtains heaved in the light breeze from the balcony, pastel rugs covered the floors, and small potted plants added a gentle touch of green everywhere. There were shelves full of books, candles, and little handwritten notes tucked between the pages.

"Where are your friends?" I asked, looking around the silent living room.

"They're usually busy with their work or off at parties." She laughed, brushing a strand of hair behind her ear.

"Why don't you join them?" I interrupted, genuinely curious.

She shook her head gently. "I somehow don't like partying or loud noise. I'm more into exploring myself, quiet moments, books, and my thoughts."

She pointed towards her room and told me to sit there while she prepared the Maggi. I stepped inside and paused. Her room was like a living diary, soft fairy lights draped along the walls, polaroid photos clipped to strings, a big window with sheer curtains allowing soft afternoon light to pour in. There was a small easel with an unfinished watercolour painting and a little handwritten note that read, "*breathe, feel, live*".

A collection of tiny trinkets sat on her bedside table: seashells, an old watch, a small wooden elephant. Every corner felt alive with her quiet spirit.

I wandered to her dresser and found a frame, a photo of her standing between her parents, their smiles bright and full of life. Just then, she entered with two steaming bowls of Maggi and caught me holding the frame.

"That's Maa and Papa," she said, her voice warm, her eyes shining with a softness that could melt any guard.

"They must be so proud of you," I said, my words coming out almost as a whisper. She looked at me and for a second, the air felt heavy with something neither of us named.

She guided me to her huge balcony, a beautiful space lined with fairy lights, hanging planters overflowing with flowers, and a cozy swing in one corner. We sat on a pair of bamboo chairs, the city skyline stretching out before us in the dusky, rain-sweetened air.

We slurped our Maggi, occasionally laughing as steam fogged up our glasses. "So… Maggi on a rainy evening," I teased. "Classic Veda move?"

She giggled. "Only with people I like," she said, quickly looking away, tucking her hair behind her ear again.

I felt a quiet warmth spread through my chest.

Then I asked softly, "Veda… the loss you had… it's something no one should ever have to face. How did you heal?"

She paused, her fingers playing with her fork, her gaze drifting out to the sky.

"When you heal without a hand, without a heart, without a human, you heal differently, you bloom differently," she said, a gentle smile curving her lips, though her eyes seemed to hold oceans behind them.

She looked out at the city lights shimmering beyond the balcony, her fingers curled lightly around her mug. "You know, Hriday," she continued softly, her voice steady yet tender, "it's important to move forward, for the people you love, and for the ones who still look at you with hope in their eyes. It's always necessary to remember the past, to honour it, but you can't let it chain you down. You need to move forward, without doubts, without looking back every second, because the ones who loved you would have wanted you to live, to breathe fully, to laugh without guilt."

She turned to me then, her eyes searching mine. "That day at Golu's place… I found Arohi and your picture," she confessed. "I don't think I've ever seen you happier than in that photo."

I felt my chest tighten as she paused.

"You know, Hriday," she said, her words flowing like a quiet prayer, "destiny has its own ways. Sometimes love stays, sometimes it leaves, but true love always wins when you truly want the other person to stay. It's not just about holding someone close; it's about setting them free too. Love is the strongest when you wish for their happiness, even if it's not beside you. That's the power of love, it shapes you, breaks you, and then rebuilds you into someone new, someone softer yet stronger."

I sat there, the rain-scented breeze brushing against us, and for the first time in what felt like lifetimes, I let my guard down. Words tumbled out of me, raw and trembling. I told her everything, about Arohi, about the nights I spent staring at the ceiling, feeling the emptiness echo in my bones, about how I used to be the boy who laughed too loudly, who believed love was a forever thing. Once she declared, "you are mine," after which I was never truly anyone else's, not even my own. I wasn't this silent, guarded person she knew today.

She listened without a single interruption, her eyes soft, her presence a quiet shelter I didn't know I needed. When I finally fell silent, breathless from the weight of all I had carried alone, she placed her hand gently on mine.

"I am always here to listen," she said, her voice barely above a whisper, "because I know how it feels to be unheard."

We sat in that fragile stillness for what felt like a lifetime. She let me feel every bit of my pain, but never let me drown in it. Slowly, she leaned back, a teasing glimmer returning to her eyes.

"It's high time now you accept the mantra to life," she said, a playful lilt in her voice.

"And what's that?" I asked, almost afraid to break the moment.

She tilted her head, her smile blooming like a quiet sunrise. "We are too full of life to be half-loved."

I felt something shift inside me then, as though the heavy, invisible armour I had been wearing for so long finally cracked open. For the first time in years, I felt lighter. The burden I had dragged behind me like a ghost felt as if it had finally loosened its grip.

"Thank you," I whispered, my voice thick.

I stood, took a shaky breath, and pulled her into a gentle side hug – a hug that felt like a thousand unsaid words, like a silent promise of new beginnings.

Then, with one last look at her, at the girl who somehow felt both like a storm and a safe harbour, I turned and left.

And as I stepped into the night, I realised I was finally breathing again.

MADHAV

I was lying on the sofa, staring at the ceiling, a goofy grin plastered on my face. Finally, I had my "Barbie-looking" girl, Sia. Yes! We were officially dating now.

Just then, the door creaked open. I jumped up the second I saw Hriday standing there, his shoulders heavy but his eyes soft.

"Bhaiiiii!" I yelled, rushing towards him and pulling him into a tight hug. "She said yes! Sia accepted my proposal!"

Hriday's face lit up, and he started laughing. We danced around the room like two kids, our laughter echoing through the house, crashing against the walls in the sweetest way. After we finally collapsed onto the sofa, breathless, I turned to him, still grinning.

"Where's Veda? Didn't she come with you?" I asked.

"She went home... she had some work," Hriday replied, but there was a strange sadness in his voice this time.

"What happened, Bhai? You okay?" I asked, my excitement fading as I saw his eyes cloud over.

"I don't know, Bhai," he sighed, running a hand through his hair. "There's something about Veda... this connection between us that I can't define. I don't want to hold on to it, but I also can't let it go. It's like... her aura is made of galaxies. She makes me feel like I could love again. She makes me believe that maybe... maybe love isn't meant to destroy me. But..."

"But?" I pushed gently, knowing there was more.

"But... I don't want her. I don't want us," he finally confessed, his voice barely a whisper. "The thought of loving someone again... it terrifies me. I'm scared of losing her before I even have her. I'm scared that if I let myself fall, I'll break all over again. That kind of emptiness... it haunts me. Just when I learned to hate, she came along.... And loved me like I had never broken. I can't do it, Bhai."

I grabbed his shoulders, forcing him to look at me.

"Bhai... it's time you take off this blindfold you've wrapped around your heart," I said firmly. "Can't you see how much she cares about you? How deeply she feels for you? I've seen it all, the way she steals glances at you when you're not looking, the way her eyes light up when she hears your name."

I paused, my voice softening. "You know, she once spent an entire evening with me just to learn more about you – what you like, what makes you smile, what breaks you. She always asks me, 'What did Hriday eat today? Did he sleep well? Did he laugh at all?' She's constantly thinking of ways to bring back that old, carefree laugh of yours, the one we all miss. She once left a book she knew you wanted on your desk with a small note, but never told you it was from her. She's been there in a hundred silent ways you never even noticed."

I shook my head, my voice rising with emotion. "Not every person is like that bitch, Hriday! You'd better understand this before it's too late."

Then, he let out a deep breath and softened his expression again. "Leave it now, Bhai... come on, tell me about Sia and you instead. Enough heavy talk for tonight," Hriday said, trying to bring a spark of light back into his eyes.

Hriday looked at me, a million emotions swirling behind his quiet gaze, and for a moment, the room felt heavy with unspoken truths. But in that shared silence, I knew he had finally heard me, maybe not with his ears, but with the heart he had tried so hard to lock away.

HRIDAY

I climbed up the stairs slowly, each step echoing in the empty corridor like a heartbeat I didn't want to hear. Outside, the night sky was drenched in rain, the city lights shimmering and bleeding into tiny rivers that ran down the windows. The world looked blurred, like an unfinished painting, and the damp breeze carried the scent of wet earth and faraway secrets.

I paused for a moment at the landing, leaning against the railing. The street below glowed with reflections, cars crawling past, their headlights slicing through the mist. Somewhere, a stray dog barked, and I could hear the faint clink of tea cups from a distant stall. Everything felt so achingly alive tonight, and yet inside me, there was a hollowness that refused to be filled.

What is this, Hriday? I asked myself. *What is this pull towards Veda?*

She is galaxies wrapped in human skin. A soft storm that makes me want to stand in the rain just to feel alive again. Every time she smiles, something inside me crumbles. Every time she looks at me with those searching eyes, I feel seen in a way I had forgotten was possible. She makes me feel like I am HOME again.

But I can't.

I'm not made for love, not anymore. Love to me is like holding a handful of water; no matter how tightly I hold on, it slips away, leaving only cold, empty fingers behind. I don't want to drown again in the kind of love that promises warmth but ends up freezing you from the inside.

I can't let Veda in. She deserves someone who can offer her all the pieces of the universe she carries inside her. Someone who won't flinch at the thought of tomorrow.

I leaned my head back, feeling the drizzle touch my face, mixing with the tears I didn't want to name.

No, Hriday. You can't do this.

I'll stop meeting her so often. I'll make excuses, build invisible walls, let the silences grow louder until they push her away. I'll slowly learn to live without the warmth of her presence, without her laughter echoing in my head when I try to sleep.

But as soon as I thought of her absence, of days without her teasing voice, evenings without her eyes searching for me, a sharp pain knotted in my chest.

How can I not see her?

I felt torn open, standing in that rain-soaked stairway. Half of me wanted to run to her right now, to confess everything, to hold her face and tell her that she feels like home. The other half was already dragging me away, whispering that love is a battlefield I wasn't ready to step onto again.

I stood there, trembling in the quiet war inside my heart. And then, with a shattering finality, I made up my mind.

No more love. Never again.

I took a deep breath, the night swallowing me whole, and I stepped into the darkness, carrying the weight of a decision that felt like it would haunt me for the rest of my life.

25 July

HRIDAY

It was a soft Sunday morning, the kind that feels like a quiet sigh after a long week. The sky was washed in gentle hues of grey, and the air smelled like wet earth from last night's rain. Maa had been insisting for weeks that we visit the nursery to get some new plants for the balcony, so today I finally agreed.

I walked alongside her, carrying the small woven basket she insisted on using, listening to her chatter about which plants need more sun and which ones would look good next to her roses.

As we stepped into the nursery, I felt an unexpected calm settle over me. Rows and rows of plants – green, fresh, hopeful, alive. My eyes wandered lazily between flowering pots and tall palms until they landed on a familiar figure, crouched down and examining a small marigold plant as if it held the universe inside it.

Veda.

She looked up, brushing a fallen leaf off her kurti, her face lighting up the second she saw us.

"Arrey! Hriday! Aunty!" she exclaimed, her smile stretching wide, her eyes sparkling even more brightly than the dew on the plants.

Before I could say anything, Maa's face lit up too. "Arey, Beta! You also love plants?" Maa asked, her voice instantly warm.

"Love? Aunty, they're my first love!" Veda laughed, her whole body moving with her words. She instantly began talking to Maa, as if they had known each other for years, discussing soil types, best times to re-pot, and how each plant has its own mood swings.

I stood there awkwardly, my heart beating a little faster at how naturally Veda blended into this part of my world, into Maa's world.

Veda turned to me suddenly, her smile turning into a gentle frown. "And you! Where have you been hiding this past week? No calls, no messages. Did you vanish into thin air?"

I opened my mouth to reply, but before I could, Maa cut in, "Oh, you must come home today! We'll have lunch together. You can help me set up the new plants."

Veda's face lit up again, and before I could protest, she nodded. "Of course, Aunty! I'd love to."

At home, she slipped into our space like sunlight through half-open blinds. She helped Maa arrange the new pots on the balcony, laughing when She got scolded for planting too deep, and laughed every time Maa gently smacked her hand away. She convinced Maa to let her keep a small money plant she claimed would bring "positive energy", and taught her how to name each plant like they were pets. I watched them from the corner of the balcony, a strange warmth pooling in my chest.

Later, we sat together on the living room floor, legs stretched out, sharing nimbu paani and leftover sweets Maa had made. Veda challenged me to a silly game: who could guess the names of the plants blindfolded by touching their leaves. I lost every single time, and she would giggle so loudly that Maa peeked in and started laughing too.

In that moment, sitting there with her and Maa, I felt a closeness I hadn't felt in years, not the suffocating weight of love, but the gentle safety of belonging.

Veda had dragged me out after days of me avoiding her texts and calls. She insisted on going to a lakeside spot she had discovered recently, a small hidden place with broken benches and overgrown wildflowers, far away from the noisy city.

We sat together on a mossy stone ledge by the water, legs dangling above the ripples. She brought two masala chai cups, still warm, and a packet of cream biscuits.

"Don't spill it, Hriday," she warned, poking me with her elbow as I almost tilted the cup.

I rolled my eyes. "I'm not a child," I muttered, but she just laughed, that carefree laugh that always somehow cracked open the tightest parts of me.

She dipped a biscuit into her chai, then pushed it towards my mouth, smudging a bit on my lip on purpose. "Messy," she teased, wiping it with her thumb, her fingers lingering for a second too long.

The air was gentle around us, the water reflecting small, trembling stars, and the moon floating above like a shy spectator to our silent conversations.

After a long pause, she suddenly looked at me, really looked, her eyes holding a softness that felt heavier than any words.

"You know, Hriday… I love spending time with you," she said, her voice almost trembling. "It's the only time I don't feel like I need to explain myself. You make everything feel… simple. Quiet. Like I can just breathe."

I felt something shift inside me, but I stayed still, letting her speak.

She looked down at her fingers, playing with the rim of her cup. "But… it bothers me so much when you just disappear. No calls, no replies… it feels like I lose a piece of myself every time you shut me out."

I wanted to say something, but the words felt too big, too sharp.

"You know what else?" she continued, her voice now softer than the breeze. "When I'm with you, I feel… safe. Like even my loudest silences make sense to you. You're the first person who made me believe that maybe… just maybe… I'm not too much."

My breath caught, but I let her finish.

"I find ease in you, Hriday. A kind of warmth I didn't know existed," she confessed, her eyes now shimmering with unspoken words. "Sometimes… I think I want more. Sometimes I imagine what it would feel like to hold your hand without hiding it behind laughter."

She paused, as if weighing whether to say more, then looked at me with a half-smile. "But it's okay. Because even if we're just… this… I'm happy. Happier than I've been in a long time."

I reached out and held her hand lightly, feeling the tremor in her fingers. "Veda… I promise. I'll stay. Maybe not in the way you want… but as your closest friend. I'll be here. Always."

She looked at me for a long time, searching my face for something I didn't know how to give. Then she laughed softly, wiping a tear from the corner of her eye with the back of her hand.

"Best friends," she said finally, as if repeating it to make herself believe it.

"Best friends," I echoed, smiling, though my heart ached with something I didn't know how to name.

We sat there a while longer, sipping the last of our chai, the silence between us glowing, almost tender. She leaned her head on my shoulder, and I let her. In that moment, I felt her warmth, her quiet hope pressing softly against my ribs.

Maybe she wished for more. Maybe someday she would. But for now, I chose to be blind to those hints, holding tightly to the safety of being her best friend, the way she deserved to have me, without the risk of breaking.

And as she sighed against me, I knew she was happy, even if only with this small piece of me.

Days turned into weeks, and before I knew it, the weight I had been dragging behind me for years began to feel a little lighter.

Veda and I started spending more time together, not because we planned it, but because it somehow felt necessary, like breathing. We met at bookstores, in tiny cafés with chipped mugs, and sometimes on my balcony, where she'd sit cross-legged on the floor, sipping chai and scribbling in her journal while I watched the city lights blink below.

We shared everything with each other, every fleeting thought, every small heartbreak, every stupid meme we came across. She'd send me voice notes at midnight about the moon or some random poetry she had just discovered. I'd send her blurry photos of stray cats I found on my way to class, captioned, *"Look, it's you when you're angry."*

She would steal my fries without asking, call me at odd hours to rant about a book ending, or show up at my door with homemade brownies just because she "felt like it". Slowly, I found myself laughing again, those deep, loud laughs that I had almost forgotten belonged to me.

With her, I wasn't the quiet, closed-off boy who flinched at love. I was just Hriday, the one who teased too much, who danced badly when the mood struck, who would stay up till 3 a.m. just to talk about nothing at all.

She taught me how to love small things again, the warmth of morning sunlight on my face, the smell of freshly brewed coffee, the soft joy of a new song played on repeat. She brought me books she thought I'd like, left sticky notes with silly jokes on my desk, and sometimes just sat beside me in silence when words weren't needed.

The more time I spent with her, the more pieces of myself I recovered, the parts I thought were lost forever. I started writing again, sketching in old notebooks, humming old songs to myself. Even Maa noticed, her eyes lighting up when she saw me laugh, and she would often whisper, "*Veda has done magic on you, Beta.*"

But even as the warmth grew between us, we never crossed the line. We stayed in that space we had quietly chosen, the space of best friends who knew each other's hearts without demanding them fully.

In those simple, endless days, I felt like I was finding my way home again. And though I knew she carried a silent hope for something more, we held on to what we had, tightly and gently, because it was enough.

Through her, I was becoming me again, the me I thought I had buried forever beneath grief and fear. And for the first time in years, I could look at my reflection and smile without flinching.

MADHAV

"Hriday… I'm more than happy," I said, choking back the emotion in my throat. "I got my *Hriday*, my *Veeru*, back. I love you, just the way you are now, Bhai." I pulled him into a tight hug, the kind that said everything words couldn't.

Hriday didn't resist.

For the first time in a long while, I saw something soften in his eyes.

"I know, Golu," he murmured. "Everything feels so light these days. Like a burden has finally lifted. I'm… beyond grateful. To you. To Veda. I don't even remember how it felt to breathe like this. I never thought I'd find that version of me again. I didn't even want to. But you both… you never gave up on me."

I smiled, eyes wet.

"Hriday… it wasn't me. It was her. It's always been her."

He looked at me, confused.

"Veda," I said gently. "She's the one who's been loving you when you couldn't love yourself. The day she saw you for the first time, I swear, something changed in her. She didn't fall for the version of you from the past. She fell for *this* you, the one who walks with wounds, the one who carries silence like a second skin. She never asked you to be someone else, Hriday. She just wanted you, as you are."

Hriday's gaze dropped to the floor.

I continued, slowly, like every word needed him to believe it.

"You know, I've seen her. The way her eyes search for you in a room. The way her voice softens when she speaks your name. The way she notices the smallest things about you, how you fiddle with your watch when you're anxious, how your hands tremble after a memory hits you. Every time she looked at you, it was with a silent wish, that you'd turn, just once, and see the way she had been loving you all along. She waited, Hriday. She stayed."

I looked him in the eye.

"Not many do."

A silence fell, heavy and meaningful. Then Hriday finally spoke, voice barely above a whisper.

"Golu… I know. I know she loves me. And... so do I. But I'm scared. I'm scared of what love did to me last time. What if Veda leaves too? What if she wakes up one day and realises I'm not enough? That I'm still broken in places she can't reach?"

I held his shoulder firmly.

"Then listen to me, Arohi and Veda are not the same. Arohi was a chapter. Veda is the story."

Hriday looked away, battling the tears, the past, the guilt.

"Veda didn't walk into your life to be another wound. She came to be the reason you start healing. She's proof that even after a storm, something beautiful can still grow. Maybe she was sent for you, Hriday. So you could live again. So you could laugh again. So you'd stop surviving, and start living."

But he didn't reply.

He sat there, silent… lost.

I could see the war behind his eyes, the pull of a past he couldn't escape and the fear of a future he didn't know how to trust.

"What if she leaves too?" he whispered, almost to himself.

"What if Arohi comes back… What if I mess everything up?"

I had no perfect answers.

So I just stayed there beside him.

Because sometimes, love isn't about answers.

It's about staying when someone's too afraid to ask you to.

And in that moment, I realised: Even the strongest hearts can be terrified of being loved again.

Six Months Later

HRIDAY

It was a slow, heavy afternoon, the kind when the air feels too thick to breathe, and even the sun seems to drag itself across the sky. I was sitting by my window, trying to read, but the words blurred together like watercolours left in the rain.

My phone buzzed once. Twice. Fifteen times. Then went quiet.

It was Veda, probably. She had been waiting to meet me, to tell me something. But today… today was tenth February… Arohi and my day. The day I asked her to be mine, and she said yes. I wish I could erase it from my memory, tear it out like a page that never belonged, but some dates… some wounds disguise themselves as memories, and no matter how much they bleed, they refuse to leave. The past felt closer today, their whispers loud in the corners of my mind. I shut my eyes and let the old memories play, the smell of her perfume, the tulips she loved, the way she'd laugh with her head thrown back.

I didn't text Veda back. I didn't have the strength.

Later that night, I heard a knock. I opened the door and found her standing there, holding an envelope. Her hair was messy from the wind, her eyes shining with something between excitement and hurt.

"Hi," she said softly. Her voice felt like a soft knock on my ribs. I nodded, stepping aside. She entered slowly, her steps unsure.

"You didn't even text. I waited… the whole day," she started, her words trembling in the air between us.

"I needed space," I said, too coldly.

She looked at me, her face falling. "Because it's tenth February today…" her voice carrying more ache than anger. "Your day with her. A date that still lives somewhere inside you, even if it kills you."

She looked away, her jaw clenched. "No matter how far you've come, that date… it still lives inside you. Like a wound that never really healed."

I didn't deny it. Couldn't. The silence swallowed us.

Veda took a shaky breath, trying to steady herself. "I get it. You loved her. But Hriday… today I had something important to share. I thought… I thought you'd want to hear it."

"It could've waited," I muttered, avoiding her eyes.

Her voice cracked then, a thin thread snapping. "No, it couldn't. Not to me."

She held up the envelope, her fingers trembling, then let it drop on the table like a final goodbye.

"I got selected for the National Young Writers' Fellowship," she said, her voice suddenly empty. "My poetry is going international. This is what I dreamed of since I was thirteen… scribbling poems on old library receipts. And I waited… for you. I wanted you to be the first to know. Because somewhere, stupidly, I thought you'd be proud. Maybe stay back to read the first draft with me. But you weren't here."

Her words felt like glass slicing through quiet water.

She turned away, her shoulders shaking, but when she looked back, her eyes held a calm I didn't understand.

"But you were busy dancing with your past," she said softly. "And I'm tired… tired of writing chapters for someone who never turns the page."

She took a step towards the door, paused, and looked at me one last time. "I built this version of myself with every word I wrote, strong, brave, and whole. And tonight, you choose her over being a bookmark in your unfinished story."

Then she left. Just like that.

The envelope sat on the table, her name printed so neatly, so full of dreams. I looked at it but didn't move. My heart felt like a room emptied too quickly, echoing with all the words we never said.

I sat there for hours, the sun slipping away, the shadows swallowing my room. I thought about how she had become my constant, the voice that pulled me out of the dark, the laughter that stitched up the broken pieces.

Yet I had pushed her away. Over and over.

A part of me wanted to run after her, to hold her and say all the words that burned inside me. But another part, the part that still belonged to my past, stayed frozen.

I stayed there until the moon rose, washing the room in cold light. And for the first time in years, I felt truly alone.

Somewhere in the night, I whispered to myself, *"Maybe in another life… when I am no longer haunted."*

But tonight, all I had was an unopened envelope and the echo of a love I wasn't brave enough to hold.

Days passed like ghosts drifting through empty rooms. Neither of us called, neither of us texted. The silence between me and Veda felt like a wall that kept growing taller each morning, brick by brick.

At first, I told myself she was just busy, that she needed space like I always did. But as the days folded into each other, a quiet dread settled into my chest. Each evening, I found myself staring at my phone, hoping her name would light up the screen. But it never did.

I realised, slowly and painfully, that I had lost her. The only person who saw me beyond my ruins, who loved me in my silences and my storms. I had pushed away the one person who dared to stay.

One night, as I sat alone in the living room, Golu burst in. He looked at me like he was seeing me for the first time, really seeing me.

"Bhai... what have you done?" he asked, his voice trembling.

I looked down at my shaking hands. "I don't know," I whispered, my throat burning.

Golu slammed the table. "She loved you, Hriday! She loved you more than anyone ever did. Do you even understand that? She stayed when no one else did. She fought for you, for your healing, for your smile. And you... you kept choosing your past over her warmth."

I couldn't hold back anymore. My voice cracked as I finally spoke, "I know, Bhai... I know I was wrong. I hurt her. Again and again. I kept shutting the door in her face when all she wanted was to sit beside me in the dark."

Golu's eyes softened, but his pain only deepened. "Do you know how many times she cried in front of me? How she asked me what more she could do to make you see her? She didn't just love you, Hriday... she *believed* in you, even when you had stopped believing in yourself."

My chest felt like it was caving in. I pressed my fists into my eyes, trying to stop the flood of tears. "I thought I was protecting her from me. From my mess. But all I did was destroy her light."

Golu placed a hand on my shoulder. "Bhai, love isn't about protecting someone by pushing them away. Love is about letting them in. You shut her out, and now... you might have lost her forever."

I broke then. The weight of all my mistakes crashed down like a storm. I sobbed – loud, aching cries I hadn't let out in years.

"I feel so empty without her, Bhai," I choked out. "She became my mornings, my evenings, my silence, my laughter. And now there's nothing. Just this... hollow echo inside me."

Golu pulled me into a hug. We stayed there, two broken boys clinging to each other in the dark. "It's not too late. We'll go to her. We'll tell her everything," he whispered.

Fuelled by a fragile hope, we rushed to Veda's apartment. My heart pounded so hard it felt like it would split open. But when we reached, Anika opened the door, her face pale and tired.

"Where is she? Please... I need to see her," I pleaded, my voice barely human. Anika looked away, her eyes welling up. "She's not here anymore, Hriday."

I felt my knees give way. I grabbed the doorframe, gasping for air. "Please, Anika… I beg you… tell me where she is. I'll fix everything. I'll bring her back. Please!"

Anika shook her head, her tears falling freely now. "You don't understand. She's gone. She needed to leave to save herself. She loved you so much it was destroying her, Hriday."

I fell to the ground, my hands clawing at the floor as if I could hold on to something real, something of her. "It's my fault. It's all my fault," I whispered, over and over, like a prayer that might undo the past.

Anika bent down, her own voice breaking. "She asked us not to tell you. She wanted to disappear quietly, just like you always did with her."

Golu knelt beside me, his hand gripping my arm, but I barely felt it. Everything was spinning, the room, the world, my heart.

Then Shivi called from behind, her voice shaking. "Hriday… come with me. There's something you need to see."

I staggered after her like a maniac. My eyes were swollen, my chest hollow. She led me into Veda's room.

It smelled like her and old books. There were sticky notes everywhere, little scribbles and poems she'd written in her moments of loneliness. Drawings of tulips and sunflowers. Sketches of me, my face, my glasses, my half-smiles.

Shivi picked up a journal and handed it to me. "She wrote this for you. Every day. Even when you didn't show up, she still wrote to you."

I opened it, my hands trembling violently. Page after page, there she was. Her love. Her ache. Her hope that one day, I'd see her, really see her.

"I waited for him today again. he never came. But I still made tea for two."

"I know he's still dancing with his sorrow, but I want to be his music one day."

"Even if he doesn't choose me, I'll still choose him in every lifetime."

"He never knew the pain of waiting… Because I never let him wait."

"I was always the one who arrived."

"Too early, too eager, too much to be HIS."

"I saw the way you looked at me when I smiled like her."

"I heard the silence in your voice when I laughed too long. I became a shadow of someone you once loved. But I'm not her. I never wanted to be."

"If I reminded you too much of her, I had to leave, so you could miss me for me."

I collapsed to the floor, pressing the journal to my chest. The grief roared inside me, tearing me apart from the inside.

"She was my home," I sobbed, my voice echoing through the empty room. "And I turned her into another past."

Shivi knelt beside me, her eyes full of a sadness too deep for words. "She loved you, Hriday. You were her everything. Even when you didn't say a word, she heard your silence. You were all she wanted."

I buried my face in my hands, screaming into the darkness of my palms.

In that moment, I realised, I hadn't just lost Veda. I had lost the last chance to be whole again. I had lost the only person who had seen me, loved me, and stayed.

And now, it was too late.

Shivi looked at me with her tear-soaked eyes, her voice soft but stronger than I had ever heard it.

"Hriday, we can't sit and stare at our wounds forever, you can't find peace by avoiding life."

Her words sliced right through me, like someone had finally torn open the last layer of my walls. My breath shook as I looked at her, desperate, broken.

"Where is she, please tell me," I pleaded, my voice more like a cry than a question.

Anika jumped in sharply, her eyes firm. "We are not supposed to say, Hriday. She left for a reason."

But Shivi didn't look at her. She kept her gaze locked on mine, her lips trembling. There was a long, loaded silence in the room. Then, in a single breath that felt like a lifetime: "Alibaug," she whispered.

I felt my entire body jolt with hope, like I had been underwater for days and finally broke the surface.

I looked up at her, my lips parting as if I could finally breathe again.

"Why?" Anika snapped, her voice cracking. "Shivi, why did you?"

But Shivi didn't even glance at her. She turned fully to me, wiping her own tears, her face resolute.

"She went to her nani's house in Alibaug. Go get her, Dumbo," she said, almost laughing through her tears.

A wild, burning energy rose inside me. I grabbed Shivi's hands, pressing them tightly, my tears mixing with hers.

"Thank you," I choked out, my heart pounding so loud I could barely hear my own words.

I shot up, stumbling towards the door, my legs shaky but alive. I wiped my tears furiously, as if erasing all my hesitation with each swipe.

"Golu! Golu!" I shouted as I ran down the stairs, my voice echoing in the building. "Bhai, book my tickets for Mumbai. Now! I don't care what it takes, the first flight out!"

Golu's voice cracked. "Hriday… what?"

"Just do it! And tell Maa everything. Tell her I'll make everything right this time!" I screamed, my voice trembling but strong, as if my soul was finally on fire.

I burst out onto the street, the wind whipping against my face, my heart thundering in my chest like a war drum. Cars, people, horns, all a blur. All I could see was her.

I hailed a cab, nearly tripping over my own feet, throwing open the door as if I was running from a burning building.

"To the airport! Fast!" I shouted, slamming the door behind me.

My hands were shaking as I texted Golu again: *I'm going to get her back. I'll bring her home this time.*

As the car sped through the night, city lights streaking past like shooting stars, I felt every beat of my heart scream her name.

This time, I wasn't going to let her slip away into the darkness. This time, I was finally choosing life, choosing her.

I boarded the flight, my mind a blur of prayers and memories. The entire journey felt like I was chasing a dream slipping through my fingers. When the plane landed in Mumbai, I ran like a madman, my heart pounding in my throat. I grabbed a cab to the ferry, the city lights smearing past like old watercolours.

On the ferry to Alibaug, the sea wind slapped my face, cold and salty, but I barely felt it. Every wave whispered her name, every splash echoing the ache inside me. My phone buzzed, a message from Shivi with the address. I kept repeating it in my head like a lifeline.

I finally reached her street and stopped in front of a beautiful farmhouse. The moonlight fell softly on its tiled roof, and the walls were painted a pale yellow, almost glowing in the night. There was a huge front garden, wild and alive, with bougainvillea crawling along the fences and an old wooden swing swaying slowly in the breeze. The house smelled like earth after rain, like stories waiting to be told.

I looked at the nameplate tremblingly, *Mrs Nenna Sharma.* I was at the right place.

I opened the small iron gate, my fingers ice cold. As I walked through the garden, the scent of jasmine and mud wrapped around me. My heart was drumming so loud it felt like it would rip open my ribs.

At the door, I pressed the bell. An old woman in a beige saree opened it. She looked at me with warm, kind eyes that held whole galaxies of stories. "Hriday?" she asked, her voice soft, almost knowing.

I stood frozen, shocked. "Yes… Aunty. How do you know me?" I stammered.

She smiled, and her eyes crinkled like old letters. "Veda has told me everything, Beta. Please come inside. I'm her nani."

"Aunty… can you please tell me where she is? I need to see her," I begged, my voice breaking.

"She's in the backyard," she said gently. "Go, Beta. Be careful. It's dark there."

I nodded, barely able to breathe. My legs felt weak as I hurried around the side of the house.

And then I saw her.

She was standing under a huge tree covered in pink and white flowers, her yellow dress glowing softly in the moonlight. The dress ended just above her knees, and the way she stood, looking up at the stars, she looked ethereal, like a painting come alive, like something I had been searching for in every dream.

In that moment, she looked more than beautiful. She looked like she had always been mine.

Without thinking, I moved forward and shook the tree with all my strength. The flowers came tumbling down like soft rain, covering her hair, her shoulders, her face. She gasped and turned around, eyes wide with shock.

"This is what you dreamed of, right?" I said, my voice trembling as I stepped closer. "The flowers falling on you when you stood below the tree."

"Hriday?" she whispered, her voice breaking, her lips parting in disbelief. "You… here?"

"Yes, me," I said, stepping even closer. My tears finally spilled, rolling down my cheeks like they had been waiting for this moment.

I fell to my knees in front of her, my forehead almost touching her hand. "I'm so sorry, Veda," I sobbed. "I was a coward. I kept dancing with my wounds when you were right here, offering me the kind of love people write novels about. You gave me something I didn't even know I was capable of, the feeling of coming home, of breathing freely again."

She tried to pull me up, but I held her hands tightly, burying my face into her palms. "You made me laugh again. You made me live again. And I kept pushing you away. I was scared to love you because I didn't want to lose you like I lost her. But in trying to protect myself, I lost you anyway."

Her tears started to fall, splashing onto my hair, our breaths tangled together.

"You were the poem I didn't know I was capable of writing," I choked. "You were the sunrise after years of darkness. And I… I'm so sorry I didn't see it sooner."

I finally looked up into her eyes, my voice almost a whisper. "Please, Veda… please let me write our story now. Let me be the one who shakes the tree for you every day. Let me be the reason you believe in love even when it's hard. I promise you, all my mornings and all my nights, every broken piece, every healed scar, they're all yours now."

She fell to her knees too, our foreheads resting against each other, sobs shaking our entire bodies. I held her face in my hands as if she might vanish again, pressing my lips to her forehead, her cheeks, her hands, everywhere, as if trying to memorise her soul through my touch.

Her voice cracked as she whispered, "I just wanted you to choose me… even once."

"I choose you, Veda," I said, crying so hard I could barely speak. "I choose you in every life, every universe, every possible version of me. Only you."

She broke then, wrapping her arms around me so tightly that it felt like she was holding my heart together piece by piece. And I held her back with everything I had, finally allowing myself to fall completely, to love her without fear.

Above us, the flowers kept drifting down, the stars watched silently, and the night carried our broken promises away. In that backyard under the big old tree, with moonlight and fallen petals all around.

Her eyes glistened with tears as she looked up at me, her voice breaking softly, "You're staying with me forever now…?"

I cupped her face gently, my own eyes wet, and whispered, "If not me… then who?"

And in that breathless moment, our lips finally met, tender, trembling, and filled with all the love we had been waiting a lifetime to share.

Between every beginning, every in-between, and every ending, there exist rare, quiet moments of pure magic...

Moments that linger in your soul long after the world has moved on. Moments that stay, when everything else fades away, and sometimes, that's all your heart truly needs.

You give all of yourself, without expecting anything in return. You love, without bargaining for more. You hold on to that single, fleeting instant as if it's enough to light up an entire lifetime.

This, this is one of those rare moments.

For me.

Acknowledgements

To my parents, thank you for standing by every decision I made, for your unwavering support, and for believing in me even on the days I didn't believe in myself.

To my Shiva, for guiding me throughout and making everything possible.

To my friends, you held my hand through every chapter of this journey. Thank you for showing up, cheering me on, and reminding me why I started.

To my best friend, my calm in the storm, the one who never let me fall apart. Thank you for being my constant and for helping me breathe life into *if NOT me then WHO?*

To everyone who believed I could do this, who hyped me up, and poured their energy into my dream, this is as much yours as it is mine.

To myself, for not giving up, for turning late nights and quiet doubts into something real. You did it.

And to every single reader holding this book, thank you for showing up. More power to your heart, your healing, and your hope. It would mean a lot if you could review the book on Instagram. Don't forget to tag @ifntme_thenwho. I'd love to read your thoughts!

About the Author

Abhipsha Pattanaik is a storyteller at heart, weaving tales of love, belonging, and resilience. Her work reflects the power of human connection and the emotions we often leave unspoken.